ANTOINE DE SAINT-EXUPÉRY

The Little Prince

WITH DRAWINGS BY THE AUTHOR

TRANSLATED FROM THE FRENCH BY KATHERINE WOODS

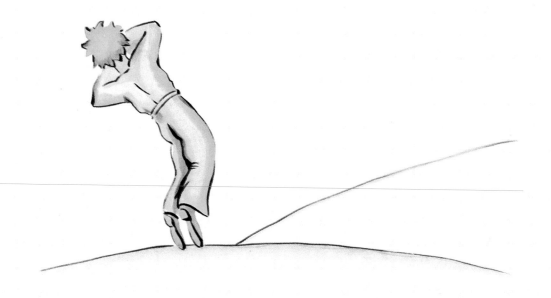

HEINEMANN · LONDON

HOW IT ALL BEGAN

*A*ll little people draw people.

We know this to be true: little people *do* draw people. Antoine de Saint-Exupéry was no exception. But what distinguishes him from other children is that he didn't stop when he grew up or rather he continued in the same vein. It isn't that grown-ups necessarily forget the pleasure of drawing but that their imagery changes. The sunset, the funny little sketch, give way to the rigid geometric lines and doodles which together with daunting columns of figures adorn the businessman's blotter. The progression of Saint-Exupéry the artist was different and it led to the meeting of two lines beneath a star, 'the loveliest and saddest landscape in the world', the closing words of this book and the crowning of a vocation discovered by the author when he was twenty-two years old. 'Now I know what I was made for: a Conté charcoal pencil!'

He had always had a feeling that this was so. It would be nice to find, amongst the scraps of paper dating from his childhood and adolescence that his family and chance have saved from oblivion, some small sketch or hint of what would later emerge as the Little Prince. But the search is in vain.

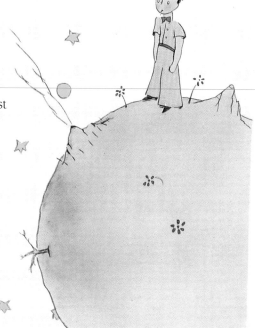

Must we conclude then that the child with the unruly golden locks appeared for the first time in 1942 in the States, the result of a meeting between the actuality of war and the memory of other times, of the pleasure of pen upon paper? It is almost impossible to find out how it all began. We can say, however, without too great a risk of contradiction, that the Little Prince did make the odd furtive appearance about seven years prior to his official presentation between the hard covers of a book. Of course, it is possible that he appeared even earlier than this, linked as he is so closely to his creator.

When I was six years old

The first introduction to the Little Prince is not as a literary character but as the little boy of six that Saint-Exupéry presents at the beginning of the book and who is none other than the author himself: 'When I was six years old . . .'

Saint-Exupéry's childhood was a comfortable one, full of games and affection. With his aunt at the Château de Saint-Maurice de Remens in the Ain département, with his grandmother in the Château de la Mole in the Var, with the love and understanding of his mother, the complicity of two older sisters, of a younger brother and even younger sister, and his governesses,

A PICTURE OF SAINT-EXUPÉRY
AS A CHILD

the equally kind and loving Paula and Moisi who will appear later in his books. What can the expression 'Little Prince' mean other than this – a child so smiled upon by fortune and circumstance?

But was this really the case? The little boy was only four when his father died. The boa constrictor had swallowed its prey. Ten years later, the First World War was declared. Three years after that he lost his younger brother François. If there was privilege, there was also sorrow, shadows to encircle the smile. It is hardly surprising that the story of the Little Prince begins with the boa constrictor and ends with the snake.

From the death of others to the death of the individual, from collective death to his own, encompassing the tribulations of the Little Prince and framed within these two references 'Once when I was six years old', the first line in the book and 'Now six years have already gone by' which mark the opening of the last chapter, we follow the story of Saint-Exupéry, told in a discreet autobiography that crosses and overshadows the realms of his imagination.

The Little Prince could have been content with a nostalgic evocation of his happy childhood, happy in spite of its griefs. But it is precisely those wounds that early on left their traces in the hand of the adolescent. This self-portrait drawn in Indian ink when he was

SELF-PORTRAIT OF SAINT-EXUPÉRY

seventeen years old is the witness. What better grasp of self, what better forerunner to the first drawings of the Little Prince than this hidden mask illuminated only by the delicate hand; this anguish pierced by light.

THE CHILD MOZART

*T*he light may not disappear for a while but the despair soon deepens. Looking for glimpses of it in the author's drawings, it is easy to forget the other little prince that Saint-Exupéry describes in *Terre des Hommes*. It is 1935. Saint-Exupéry has been sent to Moscow to write an article. His train, crossing Poland, is crammed with workers who have lost their jobs in France and are returning home. It is here, on the overnight journey, that Saint-Exupéry finds himself in the company of a young couple and their child. 'I sat facing the couple. Between the man and the woman, the child had made himself comfortable as best he could and was sleeping. But he turned in his sleep and I saw his face in the dim light of the compartment. Ah! What an angelic face. From this couple had emerged a sort of golden fruit. I leant closer to study his smooth brow, the sweet pout of the lips and I thought: this is the face of a musician, here is the child Mozart. A life full of promise. The little prince from the fairy tales . . .' 'The little prince': the character is born.

War had not yet been declared but Europe was breaking apart. And all the anxiety of the traveller was projected onto this Little Prince who would forget how to smile, towards this promise of music that would never have form. Here was Mozart assassinated.

A FAMILY PORTRAIT

THE OUTLINE OF THE LITTLE PRINCE APPEARS

*I*n 1935, the life of Saint-Exupéry is marked by two events: the accident in Libya and the first drawn appearance of the little man. There may seem to be little connection between these two events, however *The Little Prince* unites them.

On the 29th December, Saint-Exupéry, trying to make the Paris-Saigon run in record time, has to make a forced landing in the desert two hundred miles from Cairo. He then has to walk for five days before he meets, not the inhabitant of an asteroid, but a caravan of nomads who save his life. The story of the accident with the plane and the encounter in the desert is born.

For some months now, the fabulous child has acquired his face, his look and his scarf, the same one that his creator so often wears.

When he goes to restaurants, Saint-Exupéry whiles away his waiting time by

THE ACCIDENT
IN LIBYA

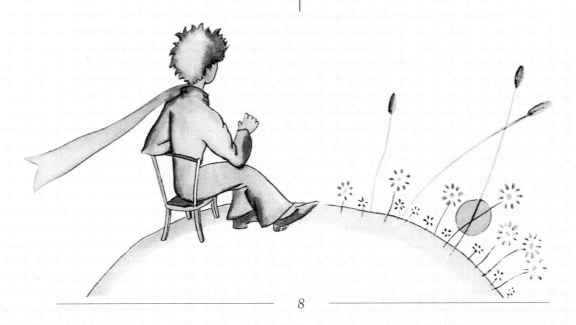

drawing pictures of a little figure on the paper tablecloth. It only requires the removal of some unnecessary wings and the accentuating of the hair for it to become the Little Prince. At about the same time, the author's letters contain at the top, at the bottom, in the margins and between the lines, that small clear familiar silhouette. The Little Prince accompanies the text or roams at random like a dislocated signature, an ironic tender clue to the identity of the correspondent.

The climate was that of war. The conflict in Spain erupted in 1936; from the Catalonian front and then a year later from that of Madrid, Saint-Exupéry sent in his dispatches to the French press. There were two short spells in Germany and then in 1939, he was called up for active service.

How the story of the accident
and the encounter originated

UNPUBLISHED WATERCOLOURS
FROM THE PIERPONT MORGAN
LIBRARY, NEW YORK

The pilot found himself committed to the struggle and the little child, his expression suddenly incensed (this drawing appears in a letter to Léon Werth dated May 1940) is drawn on a cloud, the light-hearted nature of which is belied by its fearsome inscription: Bloch 174 (a French fighter plane). The smaller cloud above it labelled Messerschmidt (a German plane) is straddled by a diminutive devil who menaces a planet tipped at a dangerous angle. It is planted with trees that foreshadow the baobabs and features an old sheep with horns and a sickly disposition, the whole illuminated at the very bottom by a rose

THE LETTER TO
LÉON WERTH

BETWEEN THE BOA CONSTRICTOR AND THE SNAKE

So, while still young, the Little Prince went off to war. Isn't this the significance of the first picture in the book that shows a boa constrictor swallowing an animal? And of the second picture, the one that so disheartened the author, and shows the boa constrictor digesting an elephant? If Antoine was six when he first imagined this, he was forty-two when he came back to it to alert us to the scandal of living civilizations falling prey to the monstrous grip of Nazism. Of the barbarous, unchecked presence that was in the process of engulfing the clumsy elephant of the West; derided but resisting with all its strength the tide of hate, murder and contempt.

Consider how, contrary to the cover and title page images, the first two pictures in the book do not show us the Little Prince. He only appears in the second chapter, standing stiffly and forlornly in his formal costume.

The first images in the book introduce us to the jungle, not the smile of a golden child.

FROM ONE JUNGLE TO ANOTHER

From the 4th September 1939 to the 5th August 1940, Saint-Exupéry's life was dominated by the war. Not as an Information Officer or a member of the *Aéronautique civil* as certain of his well-placed friends would have wished, but as a combatant. A combatant whose most famous mission was the flight to Arras that he later described in *Pilote de Guerre*.

From October 1940 on, he had the idea of going to New York. The Spanish authorities who had not forgiven him for his war reports from the Republican Front refused to allow him to cross their territory. This did not deter him. He planned to travel via Algeria and then on to Lisbon. At the end of the year, he left for the United States. He intended to stay for a few weeks only. In fact, he was there for twenty-seven months. His publishers gave him a warm welcome and in February 1939 *Terre des Hommes* was published under the title *Wind, Sand and Stars*. It was awarded the fiction prize by the Académie Française, and in the States was voted the most outstanding work of fiction in translation of the year. He was due to receive this prize in the spring of 1940. He was not there to collect it – he was flying missions over France. He received his prize a year later. 250,000 copies of the book had already been sold.

AT THE END OF THE YEAR, SAINT-EXUPÉRY LEAVES FOR NEW YORK

Was he planning a new book? He was not a prolific writer. Between 1931 and 1939 he had published *Terre des Hommes* and a few articles. So, in seven or eight weeks . . . But his experience of war made him determined to address his contemporaries: French, European, American. For this he decided to base his story on the flight to Arras. His prolonged stay allowed him to develop it and pressure from his publisher and his translator hastened its execution. And so, one year after his arrival in New York, *Pilote de Guerre* appeared. The success of *Terre des Hommes* had been considerable, that of *Pilote de Guerre* was immediate. It was top of the bestseller lists in the States for six months and, in the history of his publishing house, was the book that went most swiftly out of print. It was described as the 'most powerful response to Mein Kampf that the democracies could wish for'.

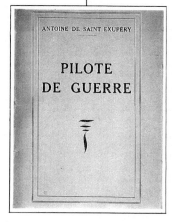

CLANDESTINE EDITION OF *PILOTE DE GUERRE* DATING FROM OCTOBER 1943

Thanks to this book, the Americans suddenly realized that France was doing its best, without adequate support, to withstand the onslaught of the German army. That the little animal was not allowing itself to be passively engulfed.

This was the beginning of a complete change in public opinion. Later than he had intended, Saint-Exupéry achieved his goal.

Once it was the child who had everything. Now it was the man who seemed to have everything. In fact, no other period in his life was so difficult. 'The pleasures of success that leave you so isolated' as he once said, the childish delight in finding his picture in the weekly magazines, of discovering his books piled high in the bookshops, none of this had the power to alleviate his gnawing anxiety. There were many reasons for his despair and it was exacerbated by the constant discomfort from his fractured limbs, the permanent pain in his kidneys and his recurrent migraines. But these physical malaises were not the main cause of his distress.

He did not like New York, and did not like the New York life style. More seriously, in spite of the attention given to *Pilote de Guerre*, he found Americans self absorbed, unable to understand the gravity of what was at stake, and that they, the greatest democracy in the world, seemed not to see that their own future was inextricably linked with the fate of others. *Pilote de Guerre* expresses this clearly but it was 1942 and there was no time for delay.

The spectacle of the division of France disturbed him even more. He came up against fixed opinions that soon became fixed in hate. The supporters of collaboration were split: for or against Pétain, for or against Laval; the supporters of resistance were likewise divided: for or against de Gaulle, for or against Giraud. What was the common ground for these exiles? It was that they all saw themselves as French, and their compatriots, caught across the Atlantic in occupied France seemed hardly to count in their eyes. Saint-Exupéry refused to align himself with any faction. He refused to support de Gaulle who would have welcomed the backing of such a prestigious figure. But this reserve, the same reserve he showed in respect of Vichy, provoked hostility from all quarters. 'Frenchmen, be reconciled in order to save your country!' he cried, lecturing in Canada and writing for the American and Canadian press on this theme. The sincerity of his voice, his noble sentiments, impress those who read his *Lettre à un otage* (Letter to a Hostage) today but then it was a language that was not welcome. This was the time for exclusivity, for invective: ecumenical thought was not in season.

IS PINK PAINT ENOUGH TO
CHANGE A MOOD?

FROM THE LITTLE MERMAID TO THE LITTLE PRINCE

*F*aced with such rejection, such an inability to understand his message, his bitterness increased. He was filled with anxiety for his family in France and for the fate of France, for the future of democracy, and he felt overwhelmed by the reaction of his compatriots, albeit fuelled by the best of intentions.

Those around him were concerned for his welfare. One day, the wife of his publisher, in order to take him out of himself, suggested he should develop the character of his little man and write a children's story about him. The Little Prince agreed to the request. But now all the tension implicit in the exercise was revealed. Creating a story in such a psychologically sombre climate could not work a therapeutic miracle. Saint-Exupéry, it seems, rushed straight off to a shop on 8th Avenue and purchased a box of watercolours. It was a promising start. But does life assume a rosy glow simply by dipping a brush into a pot of pink paint? It is true that the Little Prince retained his look of surprise, his mop of golden hair, his upright mien, but he lived in a world suffocated by war, and

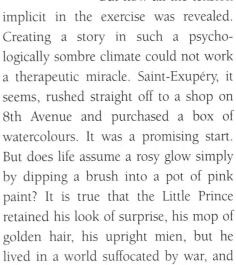

the sign under which he was born was that of death.

Don't forget: from one snake to another. Here we find the ambiguity of the first pictures in the book, of the boa constrictor and the golden child, an ambiguity that can be presented in other terms: is *The Little Prince* a story written for children or is it a meditation intended for adults?

The first interpretation is the one that accords with the wishes of his publisher; to entice him out of his melancholy by recreating the delights of childhood via a child that no disappointment can rob of his seductive grace. This wish was shared by a number of his friends and in particular by Annabella Power, the French wife of Tyrone Power. In the summer of 1941, Saint-Exupéry was admitted to hospital in Hollywood where he was staying with the film director Jean Renoir. Annabella visited him frequently and read Hans Christian Andersen's *The Little Mermaid* to him. From the Little Mermaid to the Little Prince . . . a meeting or a hint of what would follow?

The book's reception lends credibility to this hypothesis. Far from receiving the sort of acclaim that greeted the publication of *Terre des Hommes* or *Pilote de Guerre*, paradoxically *The Little Prince* tarnished the author's reputation. What sort of aberration had led this thinker, this actor in the contemporary drama to transform himself into Perrault or Grimm? He was expected to tread the boards with the New York resistance; instead he was found performing the children's puppet theatre.

It is enough to read, 'I would have preferred to begin the story like a fairy tale,' to understand that the author found this an impossibility. It is also enough to read the dedication: 'To Léon Werth. I ask the indulgence of the children who may read this book for dedicating it to a grown-up . . .'

Saint-Exupéry says he has his reasons.

And then there's his allusion to Léon Werth, when he was a little boy. The book is written for an adult who 'lives in France, where he is cold and hungry'. It is no longer possible to see the book as a

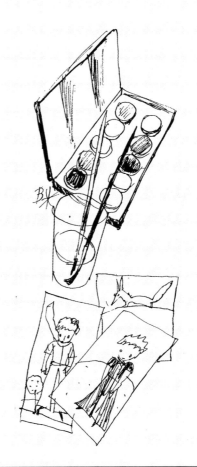

simple imaginative flight of fancy, the outcome of Saint-Exupéry's immediate circumstances. 'I don't want my book to be taken lightly,' he said. The reader is forewarned.

Not that all his readers were misled. P. L. Travers, the creator of Mary Poppins, did not deny that *The Little Prince* has its fairy tale side but as she commented, traditional fairy tales are cruel. Ann Morrow Lindberg, the wife of the pilot Charles Lindberg, immediately understood the undercurrent of nostalgia for his childhood and the haunting fear of his own death that runs through Saint-Exupéry's work.

If one attempts to read the book seriously, then one falls into another trap: to concentrate on the great themes of friendship, of having and being, of separation and closeness, the innate intelligence of things, is to reduce the fable to the level of mere fiction. To belittle the power of its imagination, to forget that the Little Prince is not old before his time, a precocious sententious little pedant but the personification of the spirit of childhood, wide-eyed and crystal-clear.

THE BOOK

The Little Prince was not created by an adult for a juvenile audience, using the device to help them to understand the world. But at the same time, it is not a tale of childhood innocence for adults with the intention of restoring to them a certain freshness of vision. These two strands become one and more besides in a story that touches us at a deeper level and that defies any sort of literary classification.

FROM THE PILOT TO THE FOX

Look at the book, allow yourself to travel from one image to the next, remembering that you are not looking at isolated pictures that accompany a story but at a drawn text that runs alongside its written counterpart, that glorifies it, stumbles over it, touches it with humour and tells its own tale that is both close and far away from the one that is developing by its side. The diversity of the individual stories is pleasing but it is also important to be open to the continuity of the preoccupations that draw them together.

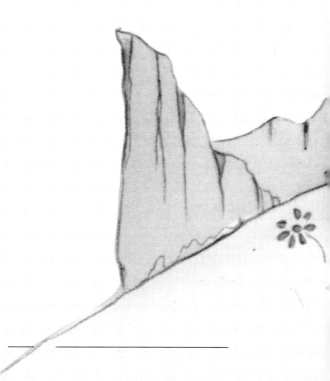

Here the art of living, a suggested system of values, and all sorts of unexpected encounters are ironically observed, all visible in the imaginative detail of the drawings. There is one point of reference that links these disparate anecdotes – the train of thought behind them. The Little Prince's behaviour is determined by need. 'If you please, draw me a sheep!' It is the first thing he says. He asks a question and the question is more important than the answer. He walks: the act of walking is more important than the destination. He desires: his longing is more important than the object of his desire. Values? Each one highlights the luxury of relationship, of the secret riches of the human spirit, of the world seen anew through the eyes of another. And to the respect that should be accorded to this richness, to this light, to the generous nature of these connections.

Although the six asteroids that the

Little Prince visits seem so different one from another, from that of the king to that of the geographer, in fact they all come from the same source. They are far-fetched? They cannot be dismissed so lightly. Each one obeys an implacable logic, so eloquently evidenced in the case of the tippler who drinks in order to forget the shame of his drinking. Saint-Exupéry does not attack anyone's stupidity. He merely reveals the constant and ruinous effects of the rational mind. Here is a rigorous coherence of thought that remains supple, does not harden into any sort of applied system and is characterized by nuance and subtlety. A pilot crashes in the desert and receives, in a miraculous encounter with a child, revelations of wisdom. A scenario from which one could fear the worst. Luckily, things are not so simple.

This is because the adult can reveal himself wise and the child perplexed. If the narrator teaches the reader, if he is often taught by the child; the child is not the source of all the wisdom. The fox will show him that. A pyramid of learning is created with the fox and his teaching at the summit. And let us not forget our last glimpse of Saint-Exupéry who dedicates the book to Léon Werth and who, once he has completed his text, takes up his pen to sketch the very last landscape. *The Little Prince* is as complex and subtle, wide-ranging and closely-knit as its approach is limpid and immediate.

A SERIES OF ORIGINAL SKETCHES
FOR THE KING

THE DRAWINGS OF THE
LITTLE PRINCE

*T*he last landscape is restricted to monochrome. When the Little Prince disappears, the star loses its brilliance. The curve of the dune no longer has its blueish tinge, that mauve-blue shadow that emphasizes the persistent power of light. The purity of a word that melts into silence, of a drawing that dissolves into the void. From the compulsive extortions of the boa constrictor to the dreadful mission of the snake, the cycle of death is complete.

Events attempt to reopen it. The Americans decide to enter the war in North Africa. The first troops land there on 4th November 1942.

On hearing the news, Saint-Exupéry intensified his efforts to rejoin the squadron with which he had flown during the French campaign from November 1939 to June 1940 and which had been transferred to Algiers. He was successful. He had just time to see *Lettre à un otage* written for Léon Werth, published in New York in February 1943. But when, two months later, *The Little Prince* appeared on the shelves, the author was on his way to the coast of Africa.

He left behind him in New York, a set of corrected galleys as well as a complete manuscript and the drawings. The collection of drawings contained rough sketches that he kept back and a number of watercolours that he put aside. For over fifty years, the latter have not been made public.

It is worth asking why the author chose not to use these watercolours. Of course, all creative work involves choice: choice that is often revealing. If the editing of a text aids comprehension,

then so will the inclusion or rejection of a drawing. The elimination of certain sketches is understandable, they were roughs and were rendered superfluous by the finished artwork. Others evidence the same trial and error quality that echoes that of the written word: the king was drawn several times and none of these was deemed acceptable. The case of the fox is more interesting. He is well executed with ears that would not draw comment. This fennec that looks like a well-bred dog lacks humour. There remain two worrying groups of drawings, one group concentrates on the pilot, the other takes up the theme of the baobabs.

THE PILOT AND THE BAOBABS

*T*he pilot-narrator is never shown in the final work. A constant presence in the text, frequently its subject, the pilot is curiously absent in the drawings. In trying to find an explanation, we can imagine that perhaps in the cast of characters – the king, the tippler, the hunter and the

THE PILOT-NARRATOR IS NEVER SHOWN
IN THE PUBLISHED WORK

The author evidently felt the same and did not retain this picture.

There are two other watercolours, both very similar, that were also put aside. They show, in the foreground, a meticulously drawn hand grasping a hammer. The drawing extends to the forearm which is abruptly cropped at the bottom of the picture. This makes the arm look as though it is emerging from the ground – Lazarus rising from his tomb – while in the middle ground, the Little Prince stands and wonders. There is plenty to ponder over. If it is simply a picture of the pilot repairing his plane under the curious gaze of his young visitor, why is the gesture so full of aggression, of menace? Anecdotal, these drawings belong to the

other walk-on parts – to which the narrator and the Little Prince clearly do not belong – there is no room for a realistic representation. The asteroid takes the place of the aeroplane which depleted of its wings, its motor, and having reached the point of perfection in its development, is cast aside.

And there again, the wonderful depiction of the child renders the inclusion of the pilot superfluous. The one drawing that includes him shows him sleeping in the desert with, in the back-ground, a broken wing and fuselage from the plane poking out of the sand, an allusion to the accident in Libya no doubt, but an incongruous presence in this conventional scene.

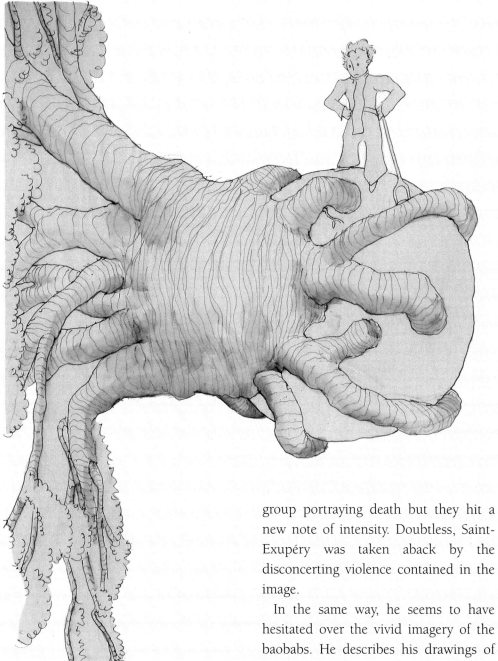

A BAOBAB? A MONSTROUS HAND WITH
GNARLED, BROKEN FINGERS

group portraying death but they hit a new note of intensity. Doubtless, Saint-Exupéry was taken aback by the disconcerting violence contained in the image.

In the same way, he seems to have hesitated over the vivid imagery of the baobabs. He describes his drawings of the baobabs as the most magnificent and most impressive of all the drawings in the book. But it is not a frightening picture. 'Your baobabs – they look a little like cabbages . . .' comments the Little Prince. But the Little Prince did not see the two pictures the author put aside. One baobab – one was enough – shorn of its leaves and clutching in its trunk and branches the asteroid; a monstrous hand with gnarled, broken fingers and mutilated claws. The fabulist has relinquished his place to the visionary; the moralist to the prophet of the apocalypse. The Little Prince has moved to another climate.

THE LEATHER STRAP

S aint-Exupéry wanted to avoid overemphasizing the dark side of a book that already had a very sombre quality to it. The period was a tragic one. Saint-Exupéry felt bitter and *The Little Prince* bears the marks of a deep pessimism. Is there then no redeeming light at the end of this story which is so alive, so ironic and so full of tenderness? In excluding his most disturbing drawings, the author preserved the tender life-enhancing happiness of his book but nevertheless the postscript is one of sadness.

The Little Prince asks the pilot to draw him a sheep: it is a famous request. Apparently the task of the sheep – the supposed benign antithesis of the boa constrictor – is to devour the dangerous sprouts of the baobabs. The sheep can as easily eat flowers.

Just like a little child, and in spite of his good intentions, the Little Prince introduces a mortal danger to his planet. His rose is in peril. Quickly the pilot draws a muzzle to restrain the predator. Things could have been left like this had not the narrator, in the last chapter of the book, suddenly become anxious – when he drew the muzzle he forgot to add the leather strap: the Little Prince would never be able to put it on the sheep.

This is really the epilogue to the story, not the death of the Little Prince. A death which foreshadows in an extraordinary way the disappearance of Saint-Exupéry on his eighth mission over France on the 31st July 1944. The epilogue is here in this missing strap. Foolishly we introduce a sheep upon our planet, foolishly we neglect to restrain it. So it is with democracies and humanism. We forget that in order to counter barbarity, be it as insidious or as inoffensive as a sheep, we must not only design muzzles but also attach the leather straps. Otherwise all our roses are in danger.

Michel Quesnel

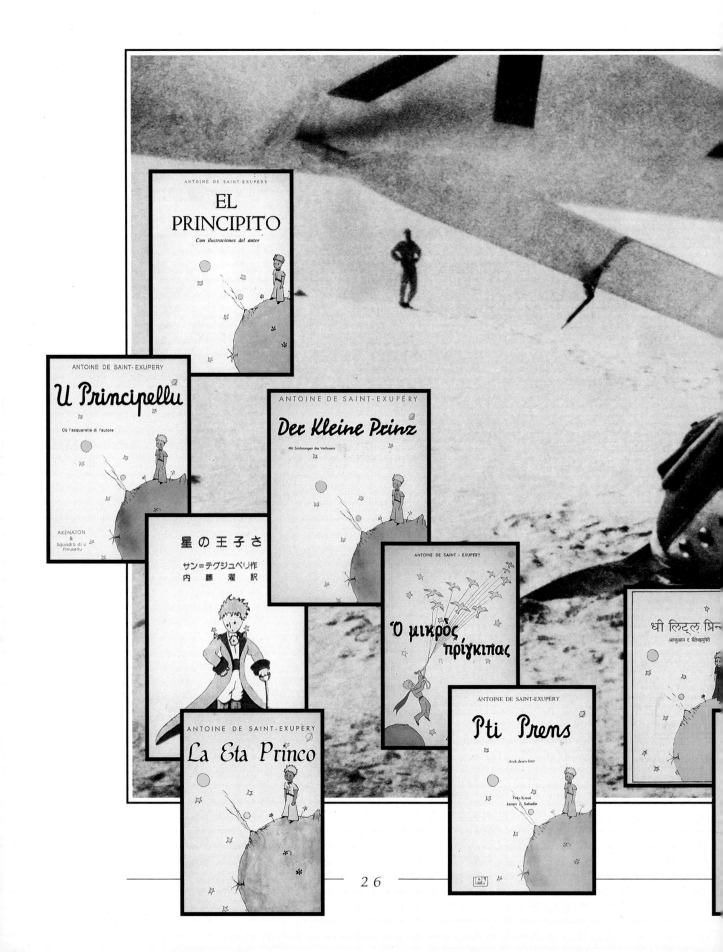

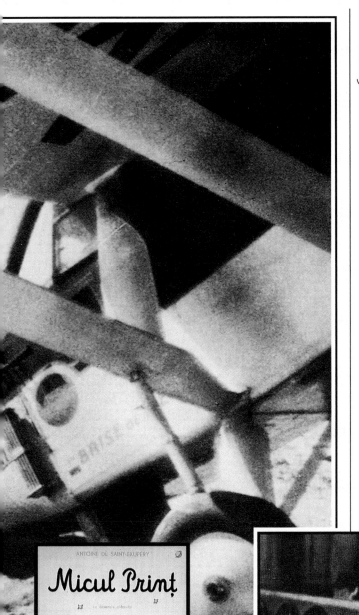

A UNIVERSAL MESSAGE

*A*ntoine de Saint-Exupéry was a humanist: he took an active interest in the fate of Humanity. *Terre des Hommes* ('Man's World'), the title of one of his books, mirrors the dream he had for Mankind. He who crossed frontiers in his plane way above the clouds, well out of the reach of barbed-wire borders, longed to create a bridge between all peoples, a direct link from heart to heart.

How could anyone claim that the heart differs according to race, religion, language or social class? Antoine de Saint-Exupéry disappeared too soon to know that his book would speak to millions of men, women and children who had, seemingly, very little in common . . . except surely the heart. And since 'only the heart is able to see what remains invisible to the eye', the message of the child with the golden hair managed to reach out and touch people all around the world.

TRANSLATED THE WORLD OVER

Blessed be the translators: without their work, the Little Prince's message would have been lost but to French children. Though language is often an obstacle and an instrument of war, it can also be an instrument of peace and brotherhood, the outstretched hand of a friend: because many translators thought it essential to make known the Little Prince's important message of quest and love, they created a chain around the world by translating it, each in his own country and own language, thus offering it to all the children who could not have understood it otherwise in the original French.

This miracle of translation* has allowed the Little Prince to cross frontiers in one hundred languages and to reach Germans, Arabs, Indians, Japanese, Israelis, Africans, Brazilians and many more. His crystal-clear laugh, his joys and sorrows, his quest for truth, his friendship with the Fox and his love for the Rose went all around the planet

Earth, nearly as fast as the sun goes around his own little planet. When two people read this book today at the same moment, then surely their two hearts beat together at the same time. And when a grown-up gives it to a child, it is doubtless to provide an excuse to read the book himself once more, to reclaim its joy and brotherhood, to become 'intelligent' again.

In roman, cyrillic, arabic, chinese and bengali characters (always accompanied by the luminous drawings of Saint-Exupéry) *The Little Prince* has been cherished, read and reread by millions of readers, adults and children, for whom the Little Prince has become a friend, perhaps even a part of themselves – a part of the heritage they will wish to pass on to those they love.

Such is probably Saint-Exupéry's greatest achievement: to allow his readers to reach, beyond the original words of this literary classic, the universality of its message. For beyond the words, and far stronger than adversity, stupidity and fear, the message is what remains and will live on.

Anne-Solange Noble

* to *translate*, like to *transfer* or to *transmit*, comes from the Latin, and means to 'bring across'.

I BELIEVE THAT FOR HIS ESCAPE HE TOOK ADVANTAGE
OF THE MIGRATION OF A FLOCK OF WILD BIRDS

A N T O I N E   D E   S A I N T - E X U P É R Y

The Little Prince

WITH DRAWINGS BY THE AUTHOR

TRANSLATED FROM THE FRENCH BY KATHERINE WOODS

HEINEMANN · LONDON

To Léon Werth

I ask the indulgence of the children who may read this book for dedicating it to a grown-up. I have a serious reason; he is the best friend I have in the world. I have another reason: this grown-up understands everything, even books about children. I have a third reason: he lives in France where he is hungry and cold. He needs cheering up. If all these reasons are not enough, I will dedicate the book to the child from whom this grown-up grew. All grown-ups were once children — although few of them remember it. And so I correct my dedication:

To Léon Werth
WHEN HE WAS A LITTLE BOY

I

*O*nce when I was six years old I saw a magnificent picture in a book, called *True Stories from Nature,* about the primeval forest. It was a picture of a boa constrictor in the act of swallowing an animal. Here is a copy of the drawing:

In the book it said: "Boa constrictors swallow their prey whole, without chewing it. After that they are not able to move, and they sleep through the six months that they need for digestion."

I pondered deeply, then, over the adventures of the jungle. And after some work with a coloured pencil I succeeded in making my first drawing. My Drawing Number One. It looked like this:

I showed my masterpiece to the grown-ups, and asked them whether the drawing frightened them. But they answered: "Frighten? Why should anyone be frightened by a hat?"

My drawing was not a picture of a hat. It was a picture of a boa constrictor digesting an elephant. But since the grown-ups were not able to understand it, I made another drawing: I drew the inside of the boa constrictor, so that the grown-ups could see it clearly. They always need to have things explained. My Drawing Number Two looked like this:

The grown-ups' response, this time, was to advise me to lay aside my drawings of boa constrictors, whether from the inside or the outside, and devote myself instead to geography, history, arithmetic and grammar. That is why, at the age of six, I gave up what might have been a magnificent career as a painter. I had been disheartened by the failure of my Drawing Number One and my Drawing Number Two. Grown-ups never understand anything by themselves, and it is tiresome for children to be always and forever explaining things to them.

So then I chose another profession, and learned to pilot aeroplanes. I have flown a little over all parts of the world; and it is true that geography has been very useful to me. At a glance I can distinguish China from Arizona. If one gets lost in the night, such knowledge is valuable.

In the course of this life I have had a great many encounters with a great many people who have been concerned with matters of consequence. I have lived a great deal among grown-ups. I have seen them intimately, close at hand. And that hasn't much improved my opinion of them.

Whenever I met one of them who seemed to me at all clear-sighted, I tried the experiment of showing him my Drawing Number One, which I have always kept. I would try to find out, so, if this was a person of true understanding. But, whoever it was, he, or she, would always say: "That is a hat."

Then I would never talk to that person about boa constrictors, or primeval forests, or stars. I would bring myself down to his level. I would talk to him about bridge, and golf, and politics, and neckties. And the grown-up would be greatly pleased to have met such a sensible man.

II

So I lived my life alone, without anyone that I could really talk to, until I had an accident with my plane in the Desert of Sahara, six years ago. Something was broken in my engine. And as I had with me neither mechanic nor any passengers, I set myself to attempt the difficult repairs all alone. It was a question of life or death for me: I had scarcely enough drinking water to last a week.

The first night, then, I went to sleep on the sand, a thousand miles from any human habitation. I was more isolated than a shipwrecked sailor on a raft in the middle of the ocean. Thus you can imagine my amazement, at sunrise, when I was awakened by an odd little voice. It said:

"If you please — draw me a sheep!"

"What!"

"Draw me a sheep!"

I jumped to my feet, completely thunderstruck. I blinked my eyes hard. I looked carefully around me. And I saw a most extraordinary small person, who stood there examining me with great seriousness. Here you may see the best portrait that, later, I was able to make of him. But my drawing is certainly very much less charming than its model.

That, however, is not my fault. The grown-ups discouraged me in my painter's career when I was six years old, and I never learned to draw anything, except boas from the outside and boas from the inside.

Now I stared at this sudden apparition with my eyes fairly starting out of my head in astonishment. Remember, I had crashed in the desert a thousand miles from any inhabited region. And yet my little man seemed neither to be straying uncertainly among the sands, nor to be fainting from fatigue or hunger or thirst or fear. Nothing about him gave any suggestion of a child lost in the middle of the desert, a thousand miles from any human habitation. When at last I was able to speak, I said to him:

"But — what are you doing here?"

And in answer he repeated, very slowly, as if he were speaking of a matter of great consequence:

"If you please — draw me a sheep . . ."

When a mystery is too overpowering, one dare not disobey. Absurd as it might seem to me, a thousand miles from any human habitation and in danger of death, I took out of my pocket a sheet of paper and my fountain-pen. But then I remembered how my studies had been concentrated on geography, history, arithmetic and grammar, and I told the little chap (a little crossly, too) that I did not know how to draw. He answered me:

"That doesn't matter. Draw me a sheep . . ."

But I had never drawn a sheep. So I drew for him one of the two pictures I had drawn so often. It was that of the boa constrictor from the outside. And I was astounded to hear the little fellow greet it with,

"No, no, no! I do not want an elephant inside a boa constrictor. A boa

HERE IS THE BEST PORTRAIT THAT, LATER,
I WAS ABLE TO MAKE OF HIM

constrictor is a very dangerous creature, and an elephant is very cumbersome. Where I live, everything is very small. What I need is a sheep. Draw me a sheep."

So then I made a drawing.

He looked at it carefully, then he said:

"No. This sheep is already very sickly. Make me another."

So I made another drawing.

My friend smiled gently and indulgently.

"You see yourself," he said, "that this is not a sheep. This is a ram. It has horns."

So then I did my drawing over once more. But it was rejected too, just like the others.

"This one is too old. I want a sheep that will live a long time."

By this time my patience was exhausted, because I was in a hurry to start taking my engine apart. So I tossed off this drawing.

And I threw out an explanation with it.

"This is only his box. The sheep you asked for is inside."

I was very surprised to see a light break over the face of my young judge:

"That is exactly the way I wanted it! Do you think that this sheep will have to have a great deal of grass?"

"Why?"

"Because where I live every-thing is very small . . ."

"There will surely be enough grass for him," I said. "It is a very small sheep that I have given you."

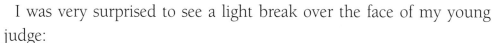

He bent his head over the drawing: "Not so small that — Look! He has gone to sleep . . ."

And that is how I made the acquaintance of the little prince.

III

It took me a long time to learn where he came from. The little prince, who asked me so many questions, never seemed to hear the ones I asked him. It was from words dropped by chance that, little by little, everything was revealed to me.

The first time he saw my aeroplane, for instance (I shall not draw my aeroplane; that would be much too complicated for me), he asked me:

"What is that object?"

"That is not an object. It flies. It is an aeroplane. It is my aeroplane."

And I was proud to have him learn that I could fly.

He cried out, then:

"What! You dropped down from the sky?"

"Yes," I answered, modestly.

"Oh! That is funny!"

And the little prince broke into a lovely peal of laughter, which irritated me very much. I like my misfortunes to be taken seriously.

Then he added:

"So you, too, come from the sky! Which is your planet?"

At that moment I caught a gleam of light in the impenetrable mystery of his presence; and I demanded, abruptly:

"Do you come from another planet?"

But he did not reply. He tossed his head gently, without taking his eyes from my plane:

"It is true that on that you can't have come from very far away . . ."

And he sank into a reverie, which lasted a long time. Then, taking my sheep out of his pocket, he buried himself in the contemplation of his treasure.

You can imagine how my curiosity was aroused by this half-confidence about the "other planets". I made a great effort, therefore, to find out more on this subject.

"My little man, where do you come from? What is this 'where I live', of which you speak? Where do you want to take your sheep?"

After a reflective silence he answered:

"The thing that is so good about the box you have given me is that at night he can use it as his house."

"That is so. And if you are good I will give you a string, too, so that you can tie him during the day; and a post to tie him to."

But the little prince seemed shocked by this offer: "Tie him! What a queer idea!"

"But if you don't tie him," I said, "he will wander off somewhere, and get lost."

My friend broke into another peal of laughter:

"But where do you think he would go?"

"Anywhere. Straight ahead of him."

Then the little prince said, earnestly: "That doesn't matter. Where I live, everything is so small!" And, with perhaps a hint of sadness, he added:

"Straight ahead of him, nobody can go very far ."

THE LITTLE PRINCE ON ASTEROID B-612

IV

$\mathcal{I}$ had thus learned a second fact of great importance: this was that the planet the little prince came from was scarcely larger than a house!

But that did not really surprise me much. I knew very well that in addition to the great planets — such as the Earth, Jupiter, Mars, Venus — to which we have given names, there are also hundreds of others, some of which are so small that one has a hard time seeing them through the telescope. When an astronomer discovers one of these he does not give it a name, but only a number. He might call it, for example, "Asteroid 325."

I have serious reason to believe that the planet from which the little prince came is the asteroid known as B-612. This asteroid has only once been seen through the telescope. That was by a Turkish astronomer, in 1909.

On making his discovery, the astronomer had presented it to the International Astronomical Congress, in a great demonstration. But he was in Turkish costume, and so nobody would believe what he said.

Grown-ups are like that . . .

Fortunately, however, for the reputation of Asteroid B-612, a Turkish dictator made a law that his subjects, under pain of death, should change to European

costume. So in 1920 the astronomer gave his demonstration all over again, dressed with impressive style and elegance. And this time everybody accepted his report.

If I have told you these details about the asteroid, and made a note of its number for you, it is on no account of the grown-ups and their ways. Grown-ups love figures. When you tell them that you have made a new friend, they never ask you any questions about

essential matters. They never say to you, "What does his voice sound like? What games does he love best? Does he collect butterflies?" Instead, they demand: "How old is he? How many brothers has he? How much does he weigh? How much money does his father make?" Only from these figures do they think they have learned anything about him.

If you were to say to the grown-ups: "I saw a beautiful house made of rosy brick, with geraniums in the windows and doves on the roof," they would not be able to get any idea of that house at all. You would have to say to them: "I saw a house that cost £4,000." They would exclaim: "Oh, what a pretty house that is!"

Just so, you might say to them: "The proof that the little prince existed is that he was charming, that he laughed, and that he was looking for a sheep. If anybody wants a sheep, that is proof that he exists." And what good would it do to tell them that? They would shrug their shoulders, and treat you like a child. But if you said to them: "The planet he came from is Asteroid B-612," then they would be convinced, and leave you in peace from their questions.

They are like that. One must not hold it against them. Children should always show great forbearance toward grown-up people.

But certainly, for us who understand life, figures are a matter of indifference. I should have liked to begin this story in the fashion of the fairy-tales. I should have liked to say: "Once upon a time there was a little prince who lived on a planet that was scarcely any bigger than himself, and who had need of a friend . . ."

To those who understand life, that would have given a much greater air of truth to my story.

For I do not want anyone to read my book carelessly. I have suffered too much grief in setting down these memories. Six years have already passed since my friend went away from me, with his sheep. If I try to describe him here, it is to make sure that I shall not forget him. To forget a friend is sad. Not everyone has had a friend. And if I forget him, I may become like the grown-ups who are no longer interested in anything but figures . . .

It is for that purpose, again, that I have bought a box of paints and some pencils. It is hard to take up drawing again at my age, when I have never made any pictures except those of the boa constrictor from the outside and the boa constrictor from the inside, since I was six. I shall certainly try to make my portraits as true to life as possible. But I am not at all sure of success. One drawing goes along all right, and another has no resemblance to its subject. I make some errors, too, in the little prince's height: in one place he is too tall and in another too short. And I feel some doubts about the colour of his costume. So I fumble along as best I can, now good, now bad, and I hope generally fair-to-middling.

In certain more important details I shall make mistakes, also. But that is something that will not be my fault. My friend never explained anything to me. He thought, perhaps, that I was like himself. But I, alas, do not know how to see sheep through the walls of boxes. Perhaps I am a little like the grown-ups. I have had to grow old.

V

As each day passed I would learn, in our talk, something about the prince's planet, his departure from it, his journey. The information would come very slowly, as it might chance to fall from his thoughts. It was in this way that I heard, on the third day, about the catastrophe of the baobabs.

This time, once more, I had the sheep to thank for it. For the little prince asked me abruptly — as if seized by a grave doubt — "It is true, isn't it, that sheep eat little bushes?"

"Yes, that is true."

"Ah! I am glad!"

I did not understand why it was important that sheep should eat little bushes. But the little prince added:

"Then it follows that they also eat baobabs?"

I pointed out to the little prince that baobabs were not little bushes, but, on the contrary, trees as big as castles; and that even if he took a whole herd of elephants away with him, the herd would not eat up one single baobab.

The idea of the herd of elephants made the little prince laugh.

"We would have to put them one on top of the other," he said.

But he made a wise comment:

"Before they grow so big, the baobabs start out by being little."

"That is strictly correct," I said. "But why do you want the sheep to eat the little baobabs?"

He answered me at once, "Oh, come, come!" as if he were speaking of something that was self-evident. And I was obliged to make a great mental effort to solve this problem, without any assistance.

Indeed, as I learned, there were on the planet where the little prince lived — as on all planets — good plants and bad plants. In consequence, there were good seeds from good plants, and bad seeds from bad plants. But seeds are invisible. They sleep deep in the heart of the earth's darkness, until some one among them is seized with the desire to awaken. Then this little seed will stretch itself and begin — timidly at first — to push a charming little sprig inoffensively upward toward the sun. If it is only a sprout of radish or the sprig of a rose-bush, one would let it grow wherever it might wish. But when it is a bad plant, one must destroy it as soon as possible, the very first instant that one recognizes it.

Now there were some terrible seeds on the planet that was the home of the little prince; and these were the seeds of the baobab. The soil of that planet was infested with them. A baobab is something you will never, never be able to get rid of if you attend to it too late. It spreads over the entire planet. It bores clear through it with its roots. And if the planet is too small, and the baobabs are too many, they split it in pieces . . .

"It is a question of discipline," the little prince said to me later on. "When you've finished your own toilet in the morning, then it is time to attend to the toilet of your planet, just so, with the greatest care. You must see to it that you pull up regularly all the baobabs, at the very first moment when they can be distinguished from the rose-bushes which they resemble so closely in their earliest youth. It is very tedious work," the little prince added, "but very easy."

And one day he said to me: "You ought to make a beautiful drawing, so that children where you live can see exactly how all this is. That would be very useful to them if they were to travel some day. Sometimes," he added, "there is no harm in putting off a piece of work until another day. But when it is a matter of baobabs, that always means a catastrophe. I knew a planet that was inhabited by a lazy man. He neglected three little bushes . . ."

So, as the little prince described it to me, I have made a drawing of that planet. I do not much like to take the tone of a moralist. But the danger of the baobabs is so little understood, and such considerable risks would be run by anyone who might get lost on an asteroid, that for once I am breaking through my reserve. "Children," I say plainly, "watch out for the baobabs!"

My friends, like myself, have been skirting this danger for a long time, without ever knowing it; and so it is for them that I have worked so hard

THE BAOBABS

over this drawing. The lesson which I pass on by this means is worth all the trouble it has cost me.

Perhaps you will ask me, "Why there are no other drawings in this book as magnificent and impressive as this drawing of the baobabs?" The reply is simple. I have tried. But with the others I have not been successful. When I made the drawing of the baobabs I was carried beyond myself by the inspiring force of urgent necessity.

VI

*O*h, little prince! Bit by bit I came to understand the secrets of your sad little life ... For a long time you had found your only entertainment in the quiet pleasure of looking at the sunset. I learned that new detail on the morning of the fourth day, when you said to me:

"I am very fond of sunsets. Come, let us go look at a sunset now."

"But we must wait," I said.

"Wait? For what?"

"For the sunset. We must wait until it is time."

At first you seemed to be very much surprised. And then you laughed to yourself. You said to me:

"I am always thinking that I am at home!"

Just so. Everybody knows that when it is noon in the United States the sun is setting over France. If you could fly to France in one minute, you could go straight into the sunset, right from noon. Unfortunately, France is too far away for that. But on your tiny planet, my little prince, all you need do is move your chair a few steps. You can see the day end

and the twilight falling whenever you like . . .

"One day," you said to me, "I saw the sunset forty-four times!"

And a little later you added:

"You know — one loves the sunset, when one is so sad . . ."

"Were you so sad, then?" I asked, "on the day of the forty-four sunsets?"

But the little prince made no reply.

VII

On the fifth day — again, as always, it was thanks to the sheep — the secret of the little prince's life was revealed to me. Abruptly, without anything to lead up to it, and as if the question had been born of long and silent meditation on his problem, he demanded:

"A sheep — if it eats little bushes, does it eat flowers, too?"

"A sheep," I answered, "eats anything it finds in its reach."

"Even flowers that have thorns?"

"Yes, even flowers that have thorns."

"Then the thorns — what use are they?"

I did not know. At that moment I was very busy trying to unscrew a bolt that had got stuck in my engine. I was very much worried, for it was becoming clear to me that the breakdown of my plane was extremely serious. And I had so little drinking water left that I had to fear the worst.

"The thorns — what use are they?"

The little prince never let go of a question, once he had asked it. As for me, I was upset over that bolt. And I answered with the first thing that came into my head:

"The thorns are of no use at all. Flowers have thorns just for spite!"

"Oh!"

There was a moment of complete silence. Then the little prince flashed back at me, with a kind of resentfulness:

"I don't believe you! Flowers are weak creatures. They are naive. They reassure themselves as best they can. They believe that their thorns are terrible weapons . . ."

I did not answer. At that instant I was saying to myself: "If this bolt still won't turn, I am going to knock it out with the hammer." Again the little prince disturbed my thoughts:

"And you actually believe that the flowers —"

"Oh, no!" I cried. "No, no, no! I don't believe anything. I answered you with the first thing that came into my head. Don't you see — I am very busy with matters of consequence!"

He stared at me, thunderstruck.

"Matters of consequence!"

He looked at me there, with my hammer in my hand, my fingers black with engine-grease, bending down over an object which seemed to him extremely ugly . . .

"You talk just like the grown-ups!"

That made me a little ashamed. But he went on, relentlessly:

"You mix everything up together . . . You confuse everything . . ."

He was really very angry. He tossed his golden curls in the breeze.

"I know a planet where there is a certain red-faced gentleman. He has never smelled a flower. He has never looked at a star. He has never loved anyone. He has never done anything in his life but add up figures. And all day he says over and over, just like you: 'I am busy with matters of consequence!' And that makes him swell up with pride. But he is not a man — he is a mushroom!"

"A what?"

"A mushroom!"

The little prince was now white with rage.

"The flowers have been growing thorns for millions of years. For millions of years the sheep have been eating them just the same. And is it not a matter of consequence to try to understand why the flowers go to so much trouble to grow thorns which are never of any use to them? Is the warfare between the sheep and the flowers not important? Is this not of more consequence than a fat red-faced gentleman's sums? And if I know — I, myself — one flower which is unique in the world, which grows nowhere but on my planet, but which one little sheep can destroy in a single bite some morning, without even noticing what he is doing — Oh! You think that is not important!"

His face turned from white to red as he continued:

"If someone loves a flower, of which just one single blossom grows in all the millions and millions of stars, it is enough to make him happy just to look at the stars. He can say to himself: 'Somewhere, my flower is there . . .' But if the sheep eats the flower, in one moment all his stars will be darkened . . . And you think that is not important!"

He could not say anything more. His words were choked by sobbing.

The night had fallen. I had let my tools drop from my hands. Of what moment now was my hammer, my bolt, or thirst, or death? On one star, one planet, my planet, the Earth, there was a little prince to be comforted. I took him in my arms, and rocked him. I said to him:

"The flower that you love is not in danger. I will draw a muzzle for your sheep. I will draw you a railing to put around your flower. I will—"

I did not know what to say to him. I felt awkward and blundering. I did not know how I could reach him, where I could overtake him and go on hand in hand with him once more.

It is such a secret place, the land of tears.

VIII

I soon learned to know this flower better. On the little prince's planet the flowers had always been very simple. They had only one ring of petals; they took up no room at all; they were a trouble to nobody. One morning they would appear in the grass, and by night they would have faded peacefully away. But one day, from a seed blown from no one knew where, a new flower had come up; and the little prince had watched very closely over this small sprout which was not like any other small sprouts on his planet. It might, you see, have been a new kind of baobab.

But the shrub soon stopped growing, and began to get ready to produce a flower. The little prince, who was present at the first appearance of a huge bud, felt at once that some sort of miraculous apparition must emerge from it. But the flower was not satisfied to complete the preparations for her beauty in the shelter of her green chamber. She chose her colours with the greatest care. She dressed herself slowly. She adjusted her petals one by one. She did not wish to go out into the world all rumpled, like the field poppies. It was only in the full radiance of her beauty that she wished to appear. Oh, yes! She was a coquettish creature! And her mysterious adornment lasted for days and days.

Then one morning, exactly at sunrise, she suddenly showed herself. And, after working with all this painstaking precision, she yawned and said: "Ah! I am scarcely awake. I beg that you

will excuse me. My petals are still all disarranged . . ."

But the little prince could not restrain his admiration: "Oh! How beautiful you are!"

"Am I not?" the flower responded, sweetly. "And I was born at the same moment as the sun . . ."

The little prince could guess easily enough that she was not any too modest — but how moving — and exciting — she was!

"I think it is time for breakfast," she added an instant later. "If you would have the kindness to think of my needs — "

And the little prince, completely abashed, went to look for a sprinkling-can of fresh water. So, he tended the flower.

So, too, she began very quickly to torment him with her vanity — which was, if the truth be known, a little difficult to deal with.

One day, for instance, when she was speaking of her four thorns, she said to the little prince: "Let the tigers come with their claws!"

"There are no tigers on my planet," the little prince objected. "And, anyway, tigers do not eat weeds."

"I am not a weed," the flower replied, sweetly.

"Please excuse me . . ."

"I am not at all afraid of tigers," she went on, "but I have a horror of draughts. I suppose you wouldn't have a screen for me?"

"A horror of draughts — that is bad luck, for a plant," remarked the little prince, and added to himself, "This flower is a very complex creature."

"At night I want you to put me under a glass globe. It is very cold where you live. In the place where I came from — "

But she interrupted herself at that point. She had come in the form of a seed. She could not have known anything of any other worlds. Embarrassed over having let herself be caught on the verge of such a naive untruth, she coughed two or three times, in order to put the little prince in the wrong.

"The screen?"

"I was just going to look for it when you spoke to me . . ."

Then she forced her cough a little more so that he should suffer from remorse just the same.

So the little prince, in spite of all the good will that was inseparable from his love, had soon come to doubt her. He had taken seriously words which were without importance, and it made him very unhappy.

"I ought not to have listened to her," he confided to me one day. "One never ought to listen to the flowers. One should simply look at them and breathe their fragrance. Mine perfumed all my planet. But I did not know how to take pleasure in all her grace. This tale of claws, which disturbed me so much, should only have filled my heart with tenderness and pity."

And he continued his confidences:

"The fact is that I did not know how to understand anything! I ought to have judged by deeds and not by words. She cast her fragrance and her radiance over me. I ought never to have run away from her . . . I ought to have guessed all the affection that lay behind her poor little stratagems. Flowers are so inconsistent! But I was too young to know how to love her . . ."

IX

I believe that for his escape he took advantage of the migration of a flock of wild birds. On the morning of his departure he put his planet in perfect order. He carefully cleaned out his active volcanoes. He possessed two active volcanoes; and they were very convenient for heating his breakfast in the morning. He also had one volcano that was extinct. But, as he said, "One never knows!" So he cleaned out the extinct volcano, too. If they are well cleaned out, volcanoes burn slowly and steadily, without any eruptions. Volcanic eruptions are like fires in a chimney.

On our earth we are obviously much too small to clean out our volcanoes. That is why they bring no end of trouble upon us.

The little prince also pulled up, with a certain sense of dejection, the last little shoots of the baobabs. He believed that he would never want to return. But on this last morning all these familiar tasks seemed very precious to him. And when he watered the flower for the last time, and prepared to place her under the shelter of her glass globe, he realized that he was very close to tears.

"Goodbye," he said to the flower.

But she made no answer.

"Goodbye," he said again.

The flower coughed. But it was not because she had a cold.

"I have been silly," she said to him, at last. "I ask your forgiveness. Try to be happy . . ."

He was surprised by this absence of reproaches. He stood there all bewildered, the glass globe held arrested in mid-air. He did not understand this quiet sweetness.

HE CAREFULLY CLEANED OUT HIS ACTIVE VOLCANOES

"Of course I love you," the flower said to him. "It is my fault that you have not known it all the while. That is of no importance. But you — you have been just as foolish as I. Try to be happy . . . Let the glass globe be. I don't want it any more."

"But the wind —"

"My cold is not so bad as all that . . . The cool night air will do me good. I am a flower."

"But the animals —"

"Well, I must endure the presence of two or three caterpillars if I wish to become acquainted with the butterflies. It seems that they are very beautiful. And if not the butterflies — and the caterpillars — who will call upon me? You will be far away . . . As for the large animals — I am not at all afraid of any of them. I have my claws."

And, naively, she showed her four thorns. Then she added:

"Don't linger like this. You have decided to go away. Now go!"

For she did not want him to see her crying. She was such a proud flower . . .

X

*H*e found himself in the neighbourhood of the asteroids 325, 326, 327, 328, 329, and 330. He began, therefore, by visiting them, in order to add to his knowledge.

The first of them was inhabited by a king. Clad in royal purple and ermine, he was seated upon a throne which was at the same time both simple and majestic.

"Ah! Here is a subject," exclaimed the king, when he saw the little prince coming.

And the little prince asked himself: "How could he recognize me when he had never seen me before?" He did not know how the world is simplified for kings. To them, all men are subjects.

"Approach, so that I may see you better," said the king, who felt consumingly proud of being at last a king over somebody.

The little prince looked everywhere to find a place to sit down; but the entire planet was crammed and obstructed by the king's magnificent ermine robe. So he remained standing upright, and, since he was tired, he yawned.

"It is contrary to etiquette to yawn in the presence of a king," the monarch said to him. "I forbid you to do so."

"I can't help it. I can't stop myself," replied the little prince, thoroughly embarrassed. "I have come on a long journey, and I have had no sleep . . ."

"Ah, then," the king said. "I order you to yawn. It is years since I have seen anyone yawning. Yawns, to me, are objects of curiosity. Come, now! Yawn again! It is an order."

"That frightens me . . . I cannot, any more . . ." murmured the little prince, now completely abashed.

"Hum! Hum!" replied the king. "Then I — I order you sometimes to yawn and sometimes to —" He spluttered a little, and seemed vexed.

For what the king fundamentally insisted upon was that his authority should be respected. He tolerated no disobedience. He was an absolute monarch. But, because he was a very good man, he made his orders reasonable.

"If I ordered a general," he would say, by way of example, "if I ordered a general to change himself into a sea bird, and if the general did not obey me, that would not be the fault of the general. It would be my fault."

"May I sit down?" came now a timid inquiry from the little prince.

"I order you to do so," the king answered him, and majestically gathered in a fold of his ermine mantle.

But the little prince was wondering ... The planet was tiny. Over what could this king really rule?

"Sire," he said to him, "I beg that you will excuse my asking you a question —"

"I order you to ask me a question," the king hastened to assure him.

"Sire — over what do you rule?"

"Over everything," said the king, with magnificent simplicity.

"Over everything?"

The king made a gesture, which took in his planet,
the other planets, and all the stars.

"Over all that?" asked the little prince.

"Over all that," the king answered.

For his rule was not only absolute: it was also universal.

"And the stars obey you?"

"Certainly they do," the king said. "They obey instantly. I do not permit insubordination."

Such power was a thing for the little prince to marvel at. If he had been master of such complete authority, he would have been able to watch the sunset, not forty-four times in one day, but seventy-two, or even a hundred, or even two hundred times, without ever having to move his chair. And because he felt a bit sad as he remembered his little planet which he had forsaken, he plucked up his courage to ask the king a favour:

"I should like to see a sunset . . . Do me that kindness . . . Order the sun to set . . ."

"If I ordered a general to fly from one flower to another like a butterfly, or to write a tragic drama, or to change himself into a sea bird, and if the general did not carry out the order that he had received, which one of us would be in the wrong?" the king demanded. "The general, or myself?"

"You," said the prince firmly.

"Exactly. One must require from each one the duty which each one can perform," the king went on. "Accepted authority rests first of all on reason. If you ordered your people to go and throw themselves into the sea, they would rise up in revolution. I have the right to require obedience because my orders are reasonable."

"Then my sunset?" the little prince reminded him: for he never forgot a question once he had asked it.

"You shall have your sunset. I shall command it. But, according to my science of government, I shall wait until conditions are favourable."

"When will that be?" inquired the little prince.

"Hum! Hum!" replied the king; and before saying anything else he consulted a bulky almanac. "Hum! Hum! That will be about — about — that will be this evening about twenty minutes to eight. And you will see how well I am obeyed!"

The little prince yawned. He was regretting his lost sunset. And then, too, he was already beginning to be a little bored.

"I have nothing more to do here," he said to the king. "So I shall set out on my way again."

"Do not go," said the king, who was very proud of having a subject. "Do not go. I will make you a Minister!"

"Minister of what?"

"Minister of — of Justice!"

"But there is nobody here to judge!"

"We do not know that," the king said to him. "I have not yet made a complete tour of my kingdom. I am very old. There is no room here for a carriage. And it tires me to walk."

"Oh, but I have looked already!" said the little prince, turning around to give one more glance to the other side of the planet. On that side, as on this, there was nobody at all . . .

"Then you shall judge yourself," the king answered. "That is the most difficult thing of all. It is much more difficult to judge oneself than to judge others. If you succeed in judging yourself rightly, then you are indeed a man of true wisdom."

"Yes," said the little prince, "but I can judge myself anywhere. I do not need to live on this planet."

"Hum! Hum!" said the king. "I have good reason to believe that somewhere on my planet there is an old rat. I hear him at night. You can judge this old rat. From time to time you will condemn him to death. Thus his life will depend on your justice. But you will pardon him on each occasion; for he must be treated thriftily. He is the only one we have."

"I," replied the little prince, "do not like to condemn anyone to death. And now I think I will go on my way."

"No," said the king.

But the little prince, having now completed his preparations for departure, had no wish to grieve the old monarch.

"If Your Majesty wishes to be promptly obeyed," he said, "he should be able to give me a reasonable order. He should be able, for example, to order me to be gone by the end of one minute. It seems to me that conditions are favourable . . ."

As the king made no answer, the little prince hesitated a moment. Then, with a sigh, he took his leave.

"I make you my Ambassador," the king called out, hastily.

He had a magnificent air of authority.

"The grown-ups are very strange," the little prince said to himself as he continued on his journey.

XI

The second planet was inhabited by a conceited man.

"Ah! Ah! I am about to receive a visit from an admirer!" he exclaimed, from afar, when he first saw the little prince coming.

For, to conceited men, all other men are admirers.

"Good morning," said the little prince. "That is a hat you are wearing."

"It is a hat for salutes," the conceited man replied. "It is to raise in salute when people acclaim me. Unfortunately, nobody at all ever passes this way."

"Yes?" said the little prince, who did not understand what the conceited man was talking about.

"Clap your hands, one against the other," the conceited man now directed him.

The little prince clapped his hands. The conceited man raised his hat in a modest salute.

"This is more entertaining than the visit to the king," the little prince said to himself. And he began again to clap his hands, one against the

other. The conceited man again raised his hat in salute.

After five minutes of this exercise the little prince grew tired of the game's monotony.

"And what should one do to make the hat come down?" he asked.

But the conceited man did not hear him. Conceited people never hear anything but praise.

"Do you really admire me very much?" he demanded of the little prince.

"What does that mean — 'admire'?"

"To admire means that you regard me as the handsomest, the best-dressed, the richest, and the most intelligent man on this planet."

"But you are the only man on your planet!"

"Do me this kindness. Admire me just the same."

"I admire you," said the little prince, shrugging his shoulders slightly, "but what is there in that to interest you so much?"

And the little prince went away.

"The grown-ups are certainly very odd," he said to himself, as he continued on his journey.

XII

The next planet was inhabited by a tippler. This was a very short visit, but it plunged the little prince into deep dejection.

"What are you doing there?" he said to the tippler, whom he found settled down in silence before a collection of empty bottles and also a collection of full bottles.

"I am drinking," replied the tippler, with a lugubrious air.

"Why are you drinking?" demanded the little prince.

"So that I may forget," replied the tippler.

"Forget what?" inquired the little prince, who already was sorry for him.

"Forget that I am ashamed," the tippler confessed, hanging his head.

"Ashamed of what?" insisted the little prince, who wanted to help him.

"Ashamed of drinking!" The tippler brought his speech to an end, and shut himself up in an impregnable silence.

And the little prince went away, puzzled.

"The grown-ups are certainly very, very odd," he said to himself, as he continued on his journey.

XIII

The fourth planet belonged to a businessman. This man was so much occupied that he did not even raise his head at the little prince's arrival.

"Good morning," the little prince said to him. "Your cigarette has gone out."

"Three and two make five. Five and seven make twelve. Twelve and three make fifteen. Good morning. Fifteen and seven make twenty-two. Twenty-two and six make twenty-eight. I haven't time to light it again. Twenty-six and five make thirty-one. Phew! Then that makes five hundred-and-one million, six-hundred-twenty-two thousand, seven-hundred-thirty-one."

"Five hundred million what?" asked the little prince.

"Eh? Are you still there? Five-hundred-and-one million — I can't stop . . . I have so much to do! I am concerned with matters of consequence. I don't amuse myself with balderdash. Two and five make seven . . ."

"Five-hundred-and-one million what?" repeated the little prince, who never in his life had let go of a question once he had asked it.

The businessman raised his head. "During the fifty-four years that I have inhabited this planet, I have been disturbed only three times. The first time was twenty-two years ago, when some giddy goose fell from goodness knows where. He made the most frightful noise that resounded all over the place, and I made four mistakes in my addition. The second time, eleven years ago, I was disturbed by an attack of rheumatism. I don't get enough exercise. I have no time for loafing. The third time — well, this is it! I was saying, then, five-hundred-and-one millions —"

"Millions of what?"

The businessman suddenly realized that there was no hope of being left in peace until he answered this question. "Millions of those little objects," he said, "which one sometimes sees in the sky."

"Flies?"

"Oh, no. Little glittering objects."

"Bees?"

"Oh, no. Little golden objects that set lazy men to idle dreaming. As for me, I am concerned with matters of consequence. There is no time for idle dreaming in my life."

"Ah! You mean the stars?"

"Yes, that's it. The stars."

"And what do you do with five-hundred millions of stars?"

"Five-hundred-and-one million, six-hundred-twenty-two thousand, seven-hundred-thirty-one. I am concerned with matters of consequence:

I am accurate."

"And what do you do with these stars?"

"What do I do with them?"

"Yes."

"Nothing. I own them."

"You own the stars?"

"Yes."

"But I have already seen a king who —"

"Kings do not *own*, they *reign over*. It is a very different matter."

"And what good does it do you to own the stars?"

"It does me the good of making me rich."

"And what good does it do you to be rich?"

"It makes it possible for me to buy more stars, if any are discovered."

"This man," the little prince said to himself, "reasons like my poor tippler." Nevertheless, he still had some more questions.

"How is it possible for one to own the stars?"

"To whom do they belong?" the businessman retorted, peevishly.

"I don't know. To nobody."

"Then they belong to me, because I was the first person to think of it."

"Is that all that is necessary?"

"Certainly. When you find a diamond that belongs to nobody, it is yours. When you discover an island that belongs to nobody, it is yours. When you get an idea before anyone else, you take out a patent on it: it is yours. So with me: I own the stars, because nobody else before me ever thought of owning them."

"Yes, that is true," said the little prince. "And what do you do with them?"

"I administer them," replied the businessman. "I count them and recount them. It is difficult. But I am a man who is naturally interested in matters of consequence."

The little prince was still not satisfied.

"If I owned a silk scarf," he said, "I could put it around my neck and take it away with me. If I owned a flower, I could pluck that flower and take it away with me. But you cannot pluck a star from heaven . . ."

"No. But I can put them in the bank."

"Whatever does that mean?"

"That means that I write the number of my stars on a little paper. And then I put this paper in a drawer and lock it with a key."

"And that is all?"

"That is enough," said the businessman.

"It is entertaining," thought the little prince. "It is rather poetic. But it is of no great consequence." On matters of consequence, the little prince had ideas which were very different from those of the grown-ups.

"I myself own a flower," he continued his conversation with the businessman, "which I water every day. I own three volcanoes, which I clean out every week (for I also clean out the one that is extinct; one never knows). It is of some use to my volcanoes, and it is of some use to my flower, that I own them. But you are of no use to the stars . . ."

The businessman opened his mouth, but he found nothing to say in answer. And the little prince went away.

"The grown-ups are certainly altogether extraordinary," he said simply, talking to himself as he continued on his journey.

XIV

*T*he fifth planet was very strange. It was the smallest of all. There was just enough room on it for a street lamp and a lamplighter. The little prince was not able to reach any explanation of the use of a street lamp and a lamplighter, somewhere in the heavens, on a planet which was so small that it had no people, and not one house. But he said to himself, nevertheless: "It may well be that this man is absurd. But he is not so absurd as the king, the conceited man, the businessman, and the tippler. For at least his work has some meaning. When he lights his street lamp, it is as if he brought one more star to life, or one flower. When he puts out his lamp, he sends the flower, or the star, to sleep. That is a beautiful occupation. And since it is beautiful, it is truly useful."

When he arrived on the planet he respectfully saluted the lamplighter.

"Good morning, sir. Why have you just put out your lamp?"

"Those are the orders," replied the lamplighter. "Good morning."

"What are the orders?"

"The orders are that I put out my lamp. Good evening." And he lighted his lamp again.

"But why have you lighted it again?"

"Those are the orders," replied the lamplighter.

"I do not understand," said the little prince.

"There is nothing to understand," said the lamplighter. "Orders are orders. Good morning." And he put out his lamp. Then he mopped his forehead with a handkerchief decorated with red squares.

"I follow a terrible profession. In the old days it was reasonable. I put the lamp out in the morning, and in the evening I lighted it again. I had the rest of the day for relaxation and the rest of the night for sleep."

"And the orders have been changed since that time?"

"The orders have not been changed," said the lamplighter. "That is the tragedy! From year to year the planet has turned more rapidly and the orders have not been changed!"

"Then what?" asked the little prince.

"Then — the planet now makes a complete turn every minute, and I no longer have a single second for repose. Once every minute I have to light my lamp and put it out!"

"That is very funny! A day lasts only one minute, here where you live!"

"It is not funny at all!" said the lamplighter. "While we have been

I FOLLOW A TERRIBLE PROFESSION

talking together a month has gone by."

"A month?"

"Yes, a month. Thirty minutes. Thirty days. Good evening." And he lighted his lamp again.

As the little prince watched him, he felt that he loved this lamplighter who was so faithful to his orders. He remembered the sunsets which he himself had gone to seek, in other days, merely by pulling up his chair; and he wanted to help his friend.

"You know," he said, "I can tell you a way you can rest whenever you want to . . ."

"I always want to rest," said the lamplighter.

For it is possible for a man to be faithful and lazy at the same time.

The little prince went on with his explanation: "Your planet is so small that three strides will take you all the way around it. To be always in the sunshine, you need only walk along rather slowly. When you want to rest, you will walk — and the day will last as long as you like."

"That doesn't do me much good," said the lamplighter. "The one thing I love in life is to sleep."

"Then you're unlucky," said the little prince.

"I am unlucky," said the lamplighter. "Good morning." And he put out his lamp.

"That man," said the little prince to himself, as he continued farther on his journey, "that man would be scorned by all the others: by the king, by the conceited man, by the tippler, by the businessman. Nevertheless he is the only one of them all who does not seem to me ridiculous. Perhaps that is because he is thinking of something else besides himself."

He breathed a sigh of regret, and said to himself again: "That man is the only one of them all whom I could have made my friend. But this planet is indeed too small. There is no room on it for two people . . ."

What the little prince did not dare confess was that he was sorry most of all to leave this planet, because it was blest every day with 1440 sunsets!

XV

*T*he sixth planet was ten times larger than the last one. It was inhabited by an old gentleman who wrote voluminous books.

"Oh, look! Here is an explorer!" he exclaimed to himself when he saw the little prince coming.

The little prince sat down on the table and panted a little. He had already travelled so much and so far!

"Where do you come from?" the old gentleman said to him.

"What is that big book?" said the little prince. "What are you doing?"

"I am a geographer," said the old gentleman.

"What is a geographer?" asked the little prince.

"A geographer is a scholar who knows the location of all the seas, rivers, towns, mountains, and deserts."

"That is very interesting," said the little prince. "Here at last is a man who has a real profession!" And he cast a look around him at the planet of the geographer. It was the most magnificent and stately planet that he had ever seen.

"Your planet is very beautiful," he said. "Has it any oceans?"

"I couldn't tell you," said the geographer.

"Ah!" The little prince was disappointed. "Has it any mountains?"

"I couldn't tell you," said the geographer.

"And towns, and rivers, and deserts?"

"I couldn't tell you that, either."

"But you are a geographer!"

"Exactly," the geographer said. "But I am not an explorer. I haven't a single explorer on my planet. It is not the geographer who goes out to count the towns, the rivers, the mountains, the seas, the oceans, and

the deserts. The geographer is much too important to go loafing about. He does not leave his desk. But he receives the explorers in his study. He asks them questions, and he notes down what they recall of their travels. And if the recollections of any one among them seem interesting to him, the geographer orders an inquiry into that explorer's moral character."

"Why is that?"

"Because an explorer who told lies would bring disaster on the books of the geographer. So would an explorer who drank too much."

"Why is that?" asked the little prince.

"Because intoxicated men see double. Then the geographer would note down two mountains in a place where there was only one."

"I know someone," said the little prince, "who would make a bad explorer."

"That is possible. Then, when the moral character of the explorer is shown to be good, an inquiry is ordered into his discovery."

"One goes to see it?"

"No that would be too complicated. But one requires the explorer to furnish proof. For example, if the discovery in question is that of a large mountain, one requires that large stones be brought back from it."

The geographer was suddenly stirred to excitement.

"But you — you come from far away! You are an explorer! You shall describe your planet to me!"

And, having opened his big register, the geographer sharpened his pencil. The recitals of explorers are put down first in pencil. One waits until the explorer has furnished proof, before putting them down in ink.

"Well?" said the geographer expectantly.

"Oh, where I live," said the little prince, "it is not very interesting. It is all so small. I have three volcanoes. Two volcanoes are active and the other is extinct. But one never knows."

"One never knows," said the geographer.

"I have also a flower."

"We do not record flowers," said the geographer.

"Why is that? The flower is the most beautiful thing on my planet!"

"We do not record them," said the geographer, "because they are ephemeral."

"What does that mean — 'ephemeral'?"

"Geographies," said the geographer, "are the books which, of all books, are most concerned with matters of consequence. They never become old-fashioned. It is very rarely that a mountain changes its position. It is very rarely that an ocean empties itself of its waters. We write of eternal things."

"But extinct volcanoes may come to life again," the little prince interrupted. "What does that mean — 'ephemeral'?"

"Whether volcanoes are extinct or alive, it comes to the same thing for us," said the geographer. "The thing that matters to us is the mountain. It does not change."

"But what does that mean — 'ephemeral'?" repeated the little prince, who never in his life had let go of a question, once he had asked it.

"It means, 'which is in danger of speedy disappearance.'"

"Is my flower in danger of speedy disappearance?"

"Certainly it is."

"My flower is ephemeral," the little prince said to himself, "and she has only four thorns to defend herself against the world. And I have left her on my planet, all alone!"

That was his first moment of regret. But he took courage once more.

"What place would you advise me to visit now?" he asked.

"The planet Earth," replied the geographer. "It has a good reputation."

And the little prince went away, thinking of his flower.

XVI

So then the seventh planet was the Earth.

The Earth is not just an ordinary planet! One can count, there, 111 kings (not forgetting, to be sure, the Negro kings among them), 7,000 geographers, 900,000 businessmen, 7,500,000 tipplers, 311,000,000 conceited men — that is to say, about 2,000,000,000 grown-ups.

To give you an idea of the size of the Earth, I will tell you that before the invention of electricity it was necessary to maintain, over the whole of the six continents, a veritable army of 462,511 lamplighters for the street lamps.

Seen from a slight distance, that would make a splendid spectacle. The movements of this army would be regulated like those of the ballet in the opera. First would come the turn of the lamplighters of New

Zealand and Australia. Having set their lamps alight, these would go off to sleep. Next, the lamplighters of China and Siberia would enter for their steps in the dance, and then they too would be waved back into the wings. After that would come the turn of the lamplighters of Russia and the Indies; then those of Africa and Europe; then those of South America; then those of North America. And never would they make a mistake in the order of their entry upon the stage. It would be magnificent.

Only the man who was in charge of the single lamp at the North Pole, and his colleague who was responsible for the single lamp at the South Pole — only these two would live free from toil and care: they would be busy twice a year.

XVII

When one wishes to play the wit, he sometimes wanders a little from the truth. I have not been altogether honest in what I have told you about the lamplighters. And I realize that I run the risk of giving a false idea of our planet to those who do not know it. Men occupy a very small space upon the Earth. If the two billion inhabitants who people its surface were all to stand upright and somewhat crowded together, as they do for some big public assembly, they could easily be put into one public square twenty miles long and twenty miles wide. All humanity could be piled up on a small Pacific islet.

The grown-ups, to be sure, will not believe you when you tell them that. They imagine that they fill a great deal of space. They fancy themselves as important as the baobabs. You should advise them, then, to make their own calculations. They adore figures, and that will please them. But do not waste your time on this extra task. It is unnecessary. You have, I know, confidence in me.

When the little prince arrived on the Earth, he was very much surprised not to see any people. He was beginning to be afraid he had come to the wrong planet, when a coil of gold, the colour of the moonlight, flashed across the sand.

"Good evening," said the little prince courteously.

"Good evening," said the snake.

"What planet is this on which I have come down?" asked the little prince.

"This is the Earth; this is Africa," the snake answered.

"Ah! Then there are no people on the Earth?"

"This is the desert. There are no people in the desert. The Earth is large," said the snake.

The little prince sat down on a stone, and raised his eyes toward the sky.

"I wonder," he said, "whether the stars are set alight in heaven so that one day each one of us may find his own again . . . Look at my planet. It is right there above us. But how far away it is!"

"It is beautiful," the snake said. "What has brought you here?"

"I have been having some trouble with a flower," said the little prince.

"Ah!" said the snake.

And they were both silent.

"Where are the men?" the little prince at last took up the conversation again. "It is a little lonely in the desert . . ."

"It is also lonely among men," the snake said.

The little prince gazed at him for a long time.

"You are a funny animal," he said at last. "You are no thicker than a finger . . ."

"But I am more powerful than the finger of a king," said the snake.

The little prince smiled.

YOU ARE A FUNNY ANIMAL . . .
YOU ARE NO THICKER THAN A FINGER

"You are not very powerful. You haven't even any feet. You cannot even travel . . ."

"I can carry you farther than any ship could take you," said the snake.

He twined himself around the little prince's ankle, like a golden bracelet.

"Whomever I touch, I send back to the earth from whence they came," the snake spoke again. "But you are innocent and true, and you come from a star . . ."

The little prince made no reply.

"You move me to pity — you are so weak on this Earth made of granite," the snake said. "I can help you, some day, if you grow too homesick for your own planet. I can —"

"Oh! I understand you very well," said the little prince. "But why do you always speak in riddles?"

"I solve them all," said the snake.

And they were both silent.

XVIII

*T*he little prince crossed the desert and met with only one flower. It was a flower with three petals, a flower of no account at all.

"Good morning," said the little prince.

"Good morning," said the flower.

"Where are the men?" the little prince asked, politely.

The flower had once seen a caravan passing.

"Men?" she echoed. "I think there are six or seven of them in existence.

I saw them, several years ago. But one never knows where to find them. The wind blows them away. They have no roots, and that makes their life very difficult."

"Goodbye," said the little prince.

"Goodbye," said the flower.

XIX

After that, the little prince climbed a high mountain. The only mountains he had ever known were the three volcanoes, which came up to his knees. And he used the extinct volcano as a foot-stool. "From a mountain as high as this one," he said to himself, "I shall be able to see the whole planet at one glance, and all the people . . ."

But he saw nothing, save peaks of rock that were sharpened like needles.

THIS PLANET IS ALTOGETHER DRY, AND ALTOGETHER POINTED

"Good morning," he said courteously.

"Good morning — Good morning — Good morning," answered the echo.

"Who are you?" said the little prince.

"Who are you — Who are you — Who are you?" answered the echo.

"Be my friends. I am all alone," he said.

"I am all alone — all alone — all alone," answered the echo.

"What a queer planet!" he thought. "It is altogether dry, and altogether pointed, and altogether harsh and forbidding. And the people have no imagination. They repeat whatever one says to them . . . On my planet I had a flower; she always was the first to speak . . ."

XX

$\mathcal{B}$ut it happened that after walking for a long time through sand, and rocks, and snow, the little prince at last came upon a road. And all roads lead to the abodes of men.

"Good morning," he said.

He was standing before a garden, all a-bloom with roses.

"Good morning," said the roses.

The little prince gazed at them. They all looked like his flower.

"Who are you?" he demanded, thunderstruck.

"We are roses," the roses said.

And he was overcome with sadness. His flower had told him that she was the only one of her kind in all the universe. And here were five thousand of them, all alike, in one single garden!

"She would be very much annoyed," he said to himself, "if she could see that . . . She would cough most dreadfully, and she would pretend that she was dying, to avoid being laughed at. And I should be obliged to pretend that I was nursing her back to life — for if I did not do that, to humble myself also, she would really allow herself to die . . ."

Then he went on with his reflections: "I thought that I was rich, with a flower that was unique in all the world; and all I had was a common rose. A common rose, and three volcanoes that come up to my knees — and one of them perhaps extinct forever . . . That doesn't make me a very great prince . . ."

And he lay down in the grass and cried.

XXI

*I*t was then that the fox appeared.

"Good morning," said the fox.

"Good morning," the little prince responded politely, although when he turned around he saw nothing.

"I am right here," the voice said, "under the apple tree."

"Who are you?" asked the little prince, and added, "You are very pretty to look at."

"I am a fox," the fox said.

"Come and play with me," proposed the little prince. "I am so unhappy."

"I cannot play with you," the fox said. "I am not tamed."

"Ah! Please excuse me," said the little prince.

But, after some thought, he added:

"What does that mean — 'tame'?"

"You do not live here," said the fox. "What is it that you are looking for?"

"I am looking for men," said the little prince. "What does that mean — 'tame'?"

"Men," said the fox. "They have guns, and they hunt. It is very disturbing. They also raise chickens. These are their only interests. Are you looking for chickens?"

"No," said the little prince. "I am looking for friends. What does that mean — 'tame'?"

"It is an act too often neglected," said the fox. "It means to establish ties."

" 'To establish ties'?"

"Just that," said the fox. "To me, you are still nothing more than a little boy who is just like a hundred thousand other little boys. And I have no need of you. And you, on your part, have no need of me. To you, I am nothing more than a fox like a hundred thousand other foxes. But if you tame me, then we shall need each other. To me, you will be unique in all the world. To you, I shall be unique in all the world . . ."

"I am beginning to understand," said the little prince. "There is a flower . . . I think that she has tamed me . . ."

"It is possible," said the fox. "On the Earth one sees all sorts of things."

"Oh, but this is not on the Earth!" said the little prince.

The fox seemed perplexed, and very curious.

"On another planet?"

"Yes."

"Are there hunters on that planet?"

"No."

"Ah, that is interesting! Are there chickens?"

"No."

"Nothing is perfect," sighed the fox.

But he came back to his idea.

"My life is very monotonous," he said. "I hunt chickens; men hunt me. All the chickens are just alike, and all men are just alike. And, in consequence, I am a little bored. But if you tame me, it will be as if the sun came to shine on my life. I shall know the sound of a step that will be different from all the others. Other steps send me hurrying back underneath the ground. Yours will call me, like music, out of my burrow. And then look: you see the grain-fields down yonder? I do not eat bread. Wheat is of no use to me. The wheat fields have nothing to say to me. And that is sad. But you have hair that is the colour of gold. Think how wonderful that will be when you have tamed me! The grain, which is also golden, will bring me back the thought of you. And

I shall love to listen to the wind in the wheat . . ."

The fox gazed at the little prince, for a long time.

"Please — tame me!" he said.

"I want to, very much," the little prince replied. "But I have not much time. I have friends to discover, and a great many things to understand."

"One only understands the things that one tames," said the fox. "Men have no more time to understand anything. They buy things all ready made at the shops. But there is no shop anywhere where one can buy friendship, and so men have no friends any more. If you want a friend, tame me . . ."

"What must I do, to tame you?" asked the little prince.

"You must be very patient," replied the fox. "First you will sit down at a little distance from me — like that — in the grass. I shall look at you out of the corner of my eye, and you will say nothing. Words are the source of misunderstandings. But you will sit a little closer to me, every day . . ."

The next day the little prince came back.

"It would have been better to come back at the same hour," said the fox. "If, for example, you came at four o'clock in the afternoon, then at three o'clock I shall begin to be happy. I shall feel happier and happier as the hour advances. At four o'clock, I shall already be worrying and jumping about. I shall show you how happy I am! But if you come at just any time, I shall never know at what hour my heart is to be ready to greet you . . . One must observe the proper rites . . ."

"What is a rite?" asked the little prince.

"Those also are actions too often neglected," said the fox. "They are what make one day different from other days, one hour from other hours. There is a rite, for example, among my hunters. Every Thursday they dance with the village girls. So Thursday is a wonderful day for me! I can take a walk as far as the vineyards. But if the hunters danced at just any time, every day would be like every other day, and I should never have any vacation at all."

IF YOU COME AT FOUR O'CLOCK IN THE AFTERNOON, THEN BY
THREE O'CLOCK I SHALL BEGIN TO BE HAPPY

So the little prince tamed the fox. And when the hour of his departure drew near —

"Ah," said the fox, "I shall cry."

"It is your own fault," said the little prince. "I never wished you any sort of harm; but you wanted me to tame you . . ."

"Yes, that is so," said the fox.

"But now you are going to cry!" said the little prince.

"Yes, that is so," said the fox.

"Then it has done you no good at all!"

"It has done me good," said the fox, "because of the colour of the wheat fields." And then he added:

"Go and look again at the roses. You will understand now that yours is unique in all the world. Then come back to say goodbye to me, and I will make you a present of a secret."

The little prince went away, to look again at the roses.

"You are not at all like my rose," he said. "As yet you are nothing. No one has tamed you, and you have tamed no one. You are like my fox when I first knew him. He was only a fox like a hundred thousand other foxes. But I have made him my friend, and now he is unique in all the world."

And the roses were very much embarrassed.

"You are beautiful, but you are empty," he went on. "One could not die for you. To be sure, an ordinary passer-by would think that my rose looked just like you — the rose that belongs to me. But in herself alone she is more important than all the hundreds of you other roses: because it is she that I have watered; because it is she that I have put under the glass globe; because it is she that I have sheltered behind the screen; because it is for her that I have killed the caterpillars (except the two or three that we saved to become butterflies); because it is she that I have listened to, when she grumbled, or boasted, or even sometimes when she said nothing. Because she is *my* rose."

And he went back to meet the fox.

"Goodbye," he said.

"Goodbye," said the fox. "And now here is my secret, a very simple secret: It is only with the heart that one can see rightly; what is essential is invisible to the eye."

"What is essential is invisible to the eye," the little prince repeated, so that he would be sure to remember.

"It is the time you have wasted for your rose that makes your rose so important."

"It is the time I have wasted for my rose —" said the little prince, so that he would be sure to remember.

"Men have forgotten this truth," said the fox. "But you must not forget it. You become responsible, forever, for what you have tamed. You are responsible for your rose . . ."

"I am responsible for my rose," the little prince repeated, so that he would be sure to remember.

AND HE LAY DOWN IN THE GRASS AND CRIED

XXII

"Good morning," said the little prince.

"Good morning," said the railway switchman.

"What do you do here?" the little prince asked.

"I sort out travellers, in bundles of a thousand," said the switchman. "I send off the trains that carry them: now to the right, now to the left."

And a brilliantly lighted express train shook the switchman's cabin as it rushed by with a roar like thunder.

"They are in a great hurry," said the little prince. "What are they looking for?"

"Not even the locomotive engineer knows that," said the switchman.

And a second brilliantly lighted express thundered by, in the opposite direction.

"Are they coming back already?" demanded the little prince.

"These are not the same ones," said the switchman. "It is an exchange."

"Were they not satisfied where they were?" asked the little prince.

"No one is ever satisfied where he is," said the switchman.

And they heard the roaring thunder of a third brilliantly lighted express.

"Are they pursuing the first travellers?" demanded the little prince.

"They are pursuing nothing at all," said the switchman. "They are asleep in there, or if they are not asleep they are yawning. Only the children are flattening their noses against the window-panes."

"Only the children know what they are looking for," said the little prince. "They waste their time over a rag doll and it becomes very important to them; and if anybody takes it away from them, they cry . . ."

"They are lucky," the switchman said.

XXIII

"Good morning," said the little prince.

"Good morning," said the merchant.

This was the merchant who sold pills that had been invented to quench thirst. You need only swallow one pill a week, and you would feel no need of anything to drink.

"Why are you selling those?" asked the little prince.

"Because they save a tremendous amount of time," said the merchant. "Computations have been made by experts. With these pills, you save fifty-three minutes in every week."

"And what do I do with those fifty-three minutes?"

"Anything you like . . ."

"As for me," said the little prince to himself, "if I had fifty-three minutes to spend as I liked, I should walk at my leisure toward a spring of fresh water."

XXIV

$\mathcal{I}$t was now the eighth day since I had had my accident in the desert, and I had listened to the story of the merchant as I was drinking the last drop of my water supply.

"Ah," I said to the little prince, "these memories of yours are very charming; but I have not yet succeeded in repairing my plane; I have nothing more to drink; and I, too, should be very happy if I could walk at my leisure toward a spring of fresh water!"

"My friend the fox —" the little prince said to me.

"My dear little man, this is no longer a matter that has anything to do with the fox!"

"Why not?"

"Because I am about to die of thirst . . ."

He did not follow my reasoning, and he answered me:

"It is a good thing to have a friend, even if one is about to die. I, for instance, am very glad to have a fox as a friend . . ."

"He has no way of guessing the danger," I said to myself. "He has never been either hungry or thirsty. A little sunshine is all that he needs . . ."

But he looked at me steadily, and replied to my thought:

"I am thirsty, too. Let us look for a well . . ."

I made a gesture of weariness. It is absurd to look for a well, at random, in the immensity of the desert. But nevertheless we started walking.

When we had trudged along for several hours, in silence, the darkness fell, and the stars began to come out. Thirst had made me a little feverish, and I looked at them as if I were in a dream. The little prince's last words came reeling back into my memory:

"Then you are thirsty, too?" I demanded.

But he did not reply to my question. He merely said to me:

"Water may also be good for the heart . . ."

I did not understand this answer, but I said nothing. I knew very well that it was impossible to cross-examine him.

He was tired. He sat down. I sat down beside him. And, after a little silence, he spoke again:

"The stars are beautiful, because of a flower that cannot be seen."

I replied, "Yes, that is so." And, without saying anything more, I looked across the ridges of sand that were stretched out before us in the moonlight.

"The desert is beautiful," the little prince added.

And that was true. I have always loved the desert. One sits down on a desert sand dune, sees nothing, hears nothing. Yet through the silence something throbs, and gleams . . .

"What makes the desert beautiful," said the little prince, "is that somewhere it hides a well . . ."

I was astonished by a sudden understanding of that mysterious radiation of the sands. When I was a little boy I lived in an old house, and legend told us that a treasure was buried there. To be sure, no one had ever known how to find it; perhaps no one had ever even looked for it. But it cast an enchantment over that house. My home was hiding a secret in the depths of its heart . . .

"Yes," I said to the little prince. "The house, the stars, the desert — what gives them their beauty is something that is invisible!"

"I am glad," he said, "that you agree with my fox."

As the little prince dropped off to sleep, I took him in my arms and set out walking once more. I felt deeply moved, and stirred. It seemed to me that I was carrying a very fragile treasure. It seemed to me, even, that there was nothing more fragile on all the Earth. In the moonlight I looked at his pale forehead, his closed eyes, his locks of hair that trembled in the wind, and I said to myself: "What I see here is nothing but a shell. What is most important is invisible . . ."

As his lips opened slightly with the suspicion of a half-smile, I said to myself, again: "What moves me so deeply about this little prince who is sleeping here, is his loyalty to a flower — the image of a rose that shines through his whole being like the flame of a lamp, even when he is asleep . . ." And I felt him to be more fragile still. I felt the need of protecting him, as if he himself were a flame that might be extinguished by a little puff of wind . . .

And, as I walked on so, I found the well, at daybreak.

XXV

"Men," said the little prince, "set out on their way in express trains, but they do not know what they are looking for. Then they rush about, and get excited, and turn round and round . . ."

And he added: "It is not worth the trouble . . ."

The well that we had come to was not like the wells of the Sahara. The wells of the Sahara are mere holes dug in the sand. This one was like a well in a village. But there was no village here, and I thought I must be dreaming . . .

"It is strange," I said to the little prince. "Everything is ready for use: the pulley, the bucket, the rope . . ."

He laughed, touched the rope, and set the pulley to working. And the pulley moaned, like an old weathervane which the wind has long since forgotten.

"Do you hear?" said the little prince. "We have wakened the well, and it is singing . . ."

HE LAUGHED, TOUCHED THE ROPE, AND SET THE PULLEY TO WORKING

I did not want him to tire himself with the rope.

"Leave it to me," I said. "It is too heavy for you."

I hoisted the bucket slowly to the edge of the well and set it there — happy, tired as I was, over my achievement. The song of the pulley was still in my ears, and I could see the sunlight shimmer in the still trembling water.

"I am thirsty for this water," said the little prince. "Give me some of it to drink . . ."

And I understood what he had been looking for.

I raised the bucket to his lips. He drank, his eyes closed. It was as sweet as some special festival treat. This water was indeed a different thing from ordinary nourishment. Its sweetness was born of the walk under the stars, the song of the pulley, the effort of my arms. It was good for the heart, like a present. When I was a little boy, the lights of the Christmas tree, the music of the Midnight Mass, the tenderness of smiling faces, used to make up, so, the radiance of the gifts I received.

"The men where you live," said the little prince, "raise five thousand roses in the same garden — and they do not find in it what they are looking for."

"They do not find it," I replied.

"And yet what they are looking for could be found in one single rose, or in a little water."

"Yes, that is true," I said.

And the little prince added:

"But the eyes are blind. One must look with the heart . . ."

I had drunk the water. I breathed easily. At sunrise the sand is the colour of honey. And that honey colour was making me happy, too. What brought me, then, this sense of grief?

"You must keep your promise," said the little prince, softly, as he sat down beside me once more.

"What promise?"

"You know — a muzzle for my sheep . . . I am responsible for this flower . . ."

I took my rough drafts of drawings out of my pocket. The little prince looked them over, and laughed as he said:

"Your baobabs — they look a little like cabbages."

"Oh!"

I had been so proud of my baobabs!

"Your fox — his ears look a little like horns; and they are too long."

And he laughed again.

"You are not fair, little prince," I said. "I don't know how to draw anything except boa constrictors from the outside and boa constrictors from the inside."

"Oh, that will be all right," he said, "children understand."

So then I made a pencil sketch of a muzzle. And as I gave it to him my heart was torn.

"You have plans that I do not know about," I said.

But he did not answer me. He said to me, instead:

"You know — my descent to the Earth . . . Tomorrow will be its anniversary."

Then, after a silence, he went on:

"I came down very near here."

And he flushed.

And once again, without understanding why, I had a queer sense of sorrow. One question, however, occurred to me:

"Then it was not by chance that on the morning when I first met you — a week ago — you were strolling along like that, all alone, a thousand miles from any inhabited region? You were on your way back to the place where you landed?"

The little prince flushed again.

And I added, with some hesitancy:

"Perhaps it was because of the anniversary?"

The little prince flushed once more. He never answered questions — but when one flushes does that not mean "Yes"?

"Ah," I said to him, "I am a little frightened —"

But he interrupted me.

"Now you must work. You must return to your engine. I will be waiting for you here. Come back tomorrow evening . . ."

But I was not reassured. I remembered the fox. One runs the risk of weeping a little, if one lets himself be tamed . . .

XXVI

Beside the well there was the ruin of an old stone wall. When I came back from my work, the next evening, I saw from some distance away my little prince sitting on top of this wall, with his feet dangling. And I heard him say:

"Then you don't remember. This is not the exact spot."

Another voice must have answered him, for he replied to it:

"Yes, yes! It is the right day, but this is not the place."

I continued my walk toward the wall. At no time did I see or hear anyone. The little prince, however, replied once again:

"— Exactly. You will see where my track begins, in the sand. You have nothing to do but wait for me there. I shall be there tonight."

I was only twenty yards from the wall, and I still saw nothing.

After a silence the little prince spoke again:

"You have good poison? You are sure that it will not make me suffer too long?"

I stopped in my tracks, my heart torn asunder; but still I did not understand.

"Now go away," said the little prince. "I want to get down from the wall."

NOW GO AWAY . . . I WANT TO GET DOWN FROM THE WALL

I dropped my eyes, then, to the foot of the wall — and I leaped into the air. There before me, facing the little prince, was one of those yellow snakes that take thirty seconds to bring your life to an end. Even as I was digging into my pocket to get out my revolver, I made a running step back. But, at the noise I made, the snake let himself flow easily across the sand like the dying spray of a fountain, and, in no apparent hurry, disappeared, with a light metallic sound, among the stones.

I reached the wall just in time to catch my little man in my arms; his face was white as snow.

"What does this mean?" I demanded. "Why are you talking with snakes?"

I had loosened the golden muffler that he always wore. I had moistened his temples, and had given him some water to drink. And now I did not dare ask him any more questions. He looked at me very gravely, and put his arms around my neck. I felt his heart beating like the heart of a dying bird, shot with someone's rifle . . .

"I am glad that you have found what was the matter with your engine," he said. "Now you can go back home —"

"How do you know about that?"

I was just coming to tell him that my work had been successful, beyond anything that I had dared to hope.

He made no answer to my question, but he added:

"I, too, am going back home today . . ."

Then, sadly —

"It is much farther . . . It is much more difficult . . ."

I realized clearly that something extraordinary was happening. I was holding him close in my arms as if he were a little child; and yet it seemed to me that he was rushing headlong toward an abyss from which I could do nothing to restrain him . . .

His look was very serious, like someone lost far away.

"I have your sheep. And I have the sheep's box. And I have the muzzle . . ."

And he gave me a sad smile.

I waited a long time. I could see that he was reviving little by little.

"Dear little man," I said to him, "You are afraid . . ."

He was afraid, there was no doubt about that. But he laughed lightly.

"I shall be much more afraid this evening . . ."

Once again I felt myself frozen by the sense of something irreparable. And I knew that I could not bear the thought of never hearing that laughter any more. For me, it was like a spring of fresh water in the desert.

"Little man," I said, "I want to hear you laugh again."

But he said to me:

"Tonight, it will be a year . . . My star, then, can be found right above the place where I came to the Earth, a year ago . . ."

"Little man," I said, "tell me that it is only a bad dream — this affair of the snake, and the meeting-place, and the star . . ."

But he did not answer my plea. He said to me, instead:

"The thing that is important is the thing that is not seen . . ."

"Yes, I know . . ."

"It is just as it is with the flower. If you love a flower that lives on a star, it is sweet to look at the sky at night. All the stars are a-bloom with flowers . . ."

"Yes, I know . . ."

"It is just as it is with the water. Because of the pulley, and the rope, what you gave me to drink was like music. You remember — how good it was."

"Yes, I know . . ."

"And at night you will look up at the stars. Where I live everything is so small that I cannot show you where my star is to be found. It is better, like that. My star will be just one of the stars, for you. And so you will love to watch all the stars in the heavens . . . They will all be your friends. And, besides, I am going to make you a present . . ."

He laughed again.

"Ah, little prince, dear little prince! I love to hear that laughter!"

"That is my present. Just that. It will be as it was when we drank the water . . ."

"What are you trying to say?"

"All men have stars," he answered, "but they are not the same things for different people. For some, who are travellers, the stars are guides. For others they are no more than little lights in the sky. For others, who are scholars, they are problems. For my businessman they are wealth. But all these stars are silent. You — you alone — will have the stars as no one else has them —"

"What are you trying to say?"

"In one of the stars I shall be living. In one of them I shall be laughing. And so it will be as if all the stars were laughing, when you look at the sky at night . . . You — only you — will have stars that can laugh!"

And he laughed again.

"And when your sorrow is comforted (time soothes all sorrows) you will be content that you have known me. You will always be my friend. You will want to laugh with me. And you will sometimes open your window, so, for that pleasure . . . And your friends will be properly astonished to see you laughing as you look up at the sky! Then you will say to them, 'Yes, the stars always make me laugh!' And they will think you are crazy. It will be a very shabby trick that I shall have played on you . . ."

And he laughed again.

"It will be as if, in place of the stars, I had given you a great number of little bells that knew how to laugh . . ."

And he laughed again. Then he quickly became serious:

"Tonight — you know . . . Do not come."

"I shall not leave you," I said.

"I shall look as if I were suffering. I shall look a little as if I were dying. It is like that. Do not come to see that. It is not worth the trouble . . ."

"I shall not leave you."

But he was worried.

"I tell you — it is also because of the snake. He must not bite you. Snakes — they are malicious creatures. This one might bite you just for fun . . ."

"I shall not leave you."

But a thought came to reassure him:

"It is true that they have no more poison for a second bite."

That night I did not see him set out on his way. He got away from me without making a sound. When I succeeded in catching up with him he was walking along with a quick and resolute step. He said to me merely:

"Ah! You are there . . ."

And he took me by the hand. But he was still worrying.

"It was wrong of you to come. You will suffer. I shall look as if I were dead; and that will not be true . . ."

I said nothing.

"You understand . . . It is too far. I cannot carry this body with me. It is too heavy."

I said nothing.

"But it will be like an old abandoned shell. There is nothing sad about old shells . . ."

I said nothing.

He was a little discouraged. But he made one more effort:

"You know, it will be very nice. I, too, shall look at the stars. All the stars will be wells with a rusty pulley. All the stars will pour out fresh water for me to drink . . ."

I said nothing.

"That will be so amusing! You will have five hundred million little bells, and I shall have five hundred million springs of fresh water . . ."

And he too said nothing more, because he was crying . . .

"Here it is. Let me go on by myself."

And he sat down, because he was afraid. Then he said, again:

"You know — my flower . . . I am responsible for her. And she is so weak! She is so naive! She has four thorns, of no use at all, to protect herself against all the world . . ."

I too sat down, because I was not able to stand up any longer.

"There now — that is all . . ."

He still hesitated a little; then he got up. He took one step. I could not move.

There was nothing there but a flash of yellow close to his ankle. He remained motionless for an instant. He did not cry out. He fell as gently as a tree falls. There was not even any sound, because of the sand.

XXVII

And now six years have already gone by . . . I have never yet told this story. The companions who met me on my return were well content to see me alive. I was sad, but I told them: "I am tired."

Now my sorrow is comforted a little. That is to say — not entirely. But I know that he did go back to his planet, because I did not find his body at

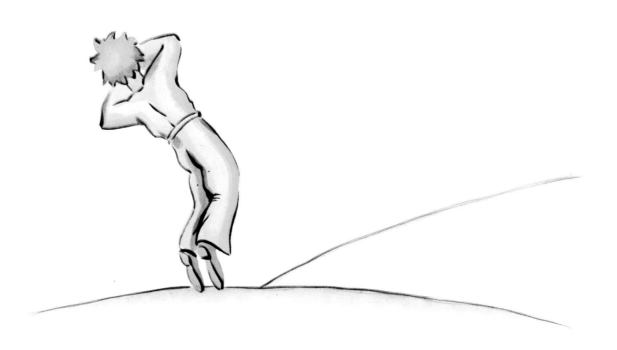

He fell as gently as a tree falls. There was not even any sound . . .

daybreak. It was not such a heavy body . . . And at night I love to listen to the stars. It is like five hundred million little bells . . .

But there is one extraordinary thing . . . When I drew the muzzle for the little prince, I forgot to add the leather strap to it. He will never have been able to fasten it on his sheep. So now I keep wondering: what is happening on his planet? Perhaps the sheep has eaten the flower . . .

At one time I say to myself: "Surely not! The little prince shuts his flower under her glass globe every night, and he watches over his sheep very carefully . . ." Then I am happy. And there is sweetness in the laughter of all the stars.

But at another time I say to myself: "At some moment or other one is absent-minded, and that is enough! On some one evening he forgot the glass globe, or the sheep got out, without making any noise, in the night . . ." And then the little bells are changed to tears . . .

Here, then, is a great mystery. For you who also love the little prince, and for me, nothing in the universe can be the same if somewhere, we do not know where, a sheep that we never saw has — yes or no? — eaten a rose . . .

Look up at the sky. Ask yourselves: Is it yes or no? Has the sheep eaten the flower? And you will see how everything changes . . .

And no grown-up will ever understand that this is a matter of so much importance!

This is, to me, the loveliest and saddest landscape in the world. It is the same as that on page 115, but I have drawn it again to impress it on your memory. It is here that the little prince appeared on Earth, and disappeared.

Look at it carefully so that you will be sure to recognize it in case you travel some day to the African desert. And, if you should come upon this spot, please do not hurry on. Wait for a time, exactly under the star. Then, if a little man appears who laughs, who has golden hair and who refuses to answer questions, you will know who he is. If this should happen, please comfort me. Send me word that he has come back.

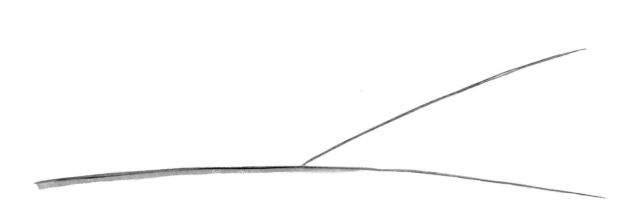

PHOTOGRAPHIC CREDITS

Archives Famille d'Agay, Paris 6, 7b, 8t, 10t, 15
Archives nationales, Paris 7t
Archives © Teledis, 9, 26
Archives Claude Werth, 11
Photo X. DR revue Icare, 13
Photos © John Phillips, 16, 21
Icare. Collection particulière.
DR Dessins de Georges Beuville, 17
Photo X, DR Collection particulière Icare
Photo X Icare, DR, 29

The Pierpont Morgan Library, New York. MA 2592;
10rtb, 20r, 20t, 22, 23tb, 24. Photography by
David A. Loggie

© The Pierpont Morgan Library and Succession
Antoine de Saint-Exupéry